IN MY SISTER'S COUNTRY

BlueHen Books

a member of Penguin Putnam Inc.

New York 2002

IN MY SISTER'S COUNTRY

Lise Haines

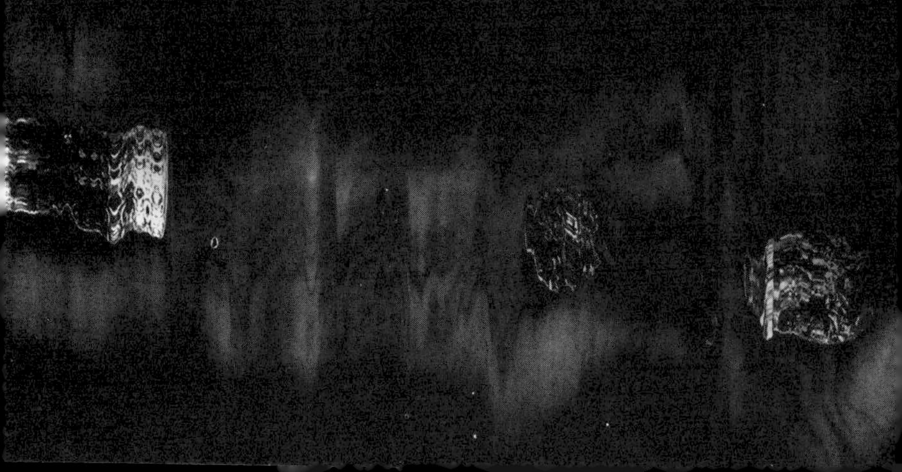

This is a work of fiction. Names, characters, places, and incidents either are the product of the author's imagination or are used fictitiously, and any resemblance to actual persons, living or dead, business establishments, events, or locales is entirely coincidental.

BlueHen Books
a member of
Penguin Putnam Inc.
375 Hudson Street
New York, NY 10014

Published simultaneously in Canada

Library of Congress Cataloging-in-Publication Data

Haines, Lise.
In my sister's country/Lise Haines.
p. cm.
ISBN 0-399-14857-4
1. Adult children of aging parents—Fiction. 2. Mothers and daughters—Fiction. 3. Hospice care—Fiction. 4. Sisters—Fiction. I. Title.
PS3608.A545 I5 2002 2001043611
813'.6—dc21

Printed in the United States of America
1 3 5 7 9 10 8 6 4 2

This book is printed on acid-free paper. ♾

Book design by Stephanie Huntwork

To Sienna, the love of my life
and the Buffalo Gals
who let us dream

and to Nort, Suzanne,
Virginia, and Irene.

For colossal heart, faith,
and hard work, I wish to thank:

Christy Fletcher, Fred Ramey,
Susan Taylor Chehak, and Kerry Tomlinson.

For their kindred spirits
and generosity, I wish to thank:

Jennifer Freed, Lyn Thompson,
Alice Kay, Barbara Guerena,
Tommy R., Margaret Desjardins,
Lane Stewart, the Mers (lym),
Johnny Seesaw, and Bennington.

We whisper still:

Zig Knoll and Kenneth Rexroth.

ONE

IN MY SISTER'S COUNTRY, *the refrigerator is filled with half-empty jars of chocolate fudge and questionable eggs; the bathtub overflows because she falls asleep while the water rises to her nostrils; bottles of dark liquor move from cabinet to cabinet around the apartment as if they're trying to run from someone; cartons of cigarettes are tucked between her hatboxes so I can steal my smokes without bothering her; three televisions are always on with the day's news, on different stations; there are deadbolts inside her bedroom door so no one can get inside while she's in there, unless they climb three flights of brick wall, up the side of the building, like the spiders that look for a warm supper in her apartment.*

—Do you have any concept of what you're doing? Amanda said one morning, throwing open the door into the guest room. I watched the doorknob dig a little deeper into the wall; she'd gotten mad before at someone sitting on that bed.

My sister wore this long, transparent nightgown, and her eyes worked themselves into a land of frenzy.

—It's a school assignment. I'm supposed to write about a family member as if they're a country, I said.

—Well, if *you're* a country, it must take the Polar Express to get there, she said. For emphasis, she went over to my window and tried to slam it shut. She had to brace her knee against the black snow on the ledge, and the cold Chicago air rippled through her gown. I heard the weights inside the frame knock against the wood, but the window barely budged.

—I told you, it's stuck. That's why I'm wearing my jacket, I said.

I wondered if Nathaniel liked that nightgown on her. I thought it was slutty. Now it had a big, black stain near one of the knees.

—Jesus Christ, Molly, there are janitors, fix-it men for this kind of thing. How many times do I have to say it? The spiders are driving me out of my mind! You have to keep the windows shut at night. During the day, you can only open the ones with screens on them.

—There *aren't* any screens.

—Because it's fucking winter! I mean, I'm digging my car out of the snow with a pickax every blessed day and you want *screens* on the window. You don't even know what season this is, do you?

She walked over to the closet and moved a rebel sweater of mine from the left side to the right so it no longer bothered her clothes.

—Don't give a shit about the heating bills, the hours put in, how often my car breaks down, what the asshole accountant said yesterday. It's just what the hell, right? Amanda's taking care of things.

I'd told her about the window, several times—and that I couldn't breathe when the heat was cranked up.

But I hadn't told her about Nathaniel.

When my sister was out of the room one night, a couple of weeks ago, he offered to give me a ride on his motorcycle sometime. It was the first time I'd run into him. Before that, I'd stayed in the guest room trying to catch a look through the keyhole. But on that particular night, I heard Amanda go off to the kitchen and I saw him lingering in the hall. Maybe he was trying to puzzle out the weird art on my sister's walls. I stepped out of the study into the hall with my back to him and pretended to fiddle with the door as if I couldn't close it. Nathaniel came up behind me. His whisper tasted like oysters and gin.

When I told him I'd think about that motorcycle ride, he slipped his fingers through my robe and into my panties, his eyelids as low as they could go without closing. Just then, Amanda called out from the kitchen. I pulled away into the study and he was gone.

—Molly! my sister shouted. I reflected her sour face back to her.

—Mom used to leave the screens on all winter, I said.

—What? You're holding *her* up to me? A woman who doesn't believe in maintenance? Like she's some kind of window-screen expert? Look, I'm not chasing the goddamn janitor down to ask him why he removes the goddamn screens in the goddamn winter, Molly. The fucking spiders are killing me! she screamed, and pulled her nightgown up so it was covering her head. She was all torso and legs and hair so black it was like blue fur. Her nipples hard stones, the appendectomy scar silver as silverfish. From her snatch to her breasts she had large red welts.

Through her nightgown, I saw her mouth move when she said: Spider bites.

She lowered her gown and threw herself into the chair in the corner, exhausted from trying to communicate with me.

—Maybe they're not spiders, I said, closing my notebook so she couldn't read what I'd written.

—They're spiders and they itch! One starts to go away and five more show up. New ones every morning. God—

She rubbed her palm over the black mark on the material—Now I'll have to throw this out, she said, calmer now.

—Maybe they're Nathaniel's.

She looked at me the way she does when I say something that makes her think of me as her little prodigy—though I'm long past the precocious age. Then she pulled a pack of cigarettes off the bookshelf and ran a hand down my hair.

—You aren't smoking these things, are you? she asked as she pushed the butts around in the ashtray, looking for something with my mark on it.

—Because I promised her you wouldn't smoke, no matter what, my sister said and struck a match. She dragged on the unfiltered tobacco. I tried to breathe in as much of the smoke as I could.

Her eyes suddenly welled up.

—I don't know what I'd do if something happened to you, she said, touching one of my knees.

She liked to tell me I had perfect knees and perfect ankles and that she hated me for them. Amanda's legs were like table-legs.

—I don't feel like work today, she said, slipping back into the loose cushions of the chair.

I looked at the family photos, the people I didn't know, on the bookshelf, surrounding Amanda—people that in all likelihood I will never know. There was the uncle my mother no longer spoke to, though I couldn't recall the story, and the tragic great-aunt who'd been crushed under a horse. My sister exhumed all of them from a box of photographs my mother didn't know what to do with; she had never identified or labeled them. In an enthusiastic moment, Amanda must have thought that their uncomfortable faces and nameless lives would make me feel at home. And then there was the picture of Amanda and me, one of the very few taken of us together.

She was seated on an unfamiliar couch in a light-filled

room, holding me in her lap. I was the passive baby, blank, unwilling, perhaps awed by sunlight. But what perplexed me was my sister's expression. She appeared to gloat as if she was happy for my arrival, but I sometimes think her face was a threat, too, a superstitious warning of things to come. Our mother liked to call Amanda a love child; Amanda liked to call me a mistake, since I came so many years after her, when things were starting to fall apart.

—Let's go downtown and take in a matinee, and then we'll just shop until dinner and then go over to Harry's and have the fattest steaks. You need some clothes, you know. You look terrible. Let's see what you're writing, she said.

—It's private, I said, pulling the notebook into my chest.

—It can't be private if you're writing it for school.

I held onto the spiral tablet as if it was my last possession, which it practically was. But she tried to wrestle it from me. Then she laughed and held out her hand.

—Give it to me, Imp. I *am* your guardian, you know.

We struggled and the tip of the metal binding gouged into one of those perfect knees of mine, raising a red line, forming a demilitarized zone. My sister finally let go and I held my palm over the shallow wound. But then she caught my other hand, the one still clutching the notebook. She took her cigarette and held it right next to my skin. Amanda was the reactive one, strictly reactive.

—Go ahead, I said.

—Just give me the notebook.

I doubled my efforts to get free. The notebook flew and my sister got it first. She sat back in her chair again. When she finished reading, she said: If I got this across my desk at work I'd tell the copy editor to throw it down the incinerator.

—My teacher says I like to get strong reactions from my readers, I said.

—You don't even understand the assignment. This has nothing to do with describing a country. There's no geography, no infrastructure, politics, social system. . . . This is self-indulgent crap, she said.

I looked for a clean T-shirt. Amanda got up from her chair and dug her fingers into her hair. This tightened the skin around her eyes until she looked like some kind of dry, clawing creature.

—Can I have ten dollars; I'm out of money, I said, while looking for my shoes under the bed.

—Maybe you can scrounge up some money selling my old fudge jars on the street.

When I looked up, I saw my sister shaking her head at my pathetic nature. She threw the notebook onto the bed and said: Show this to your teacher, bratto, and you can expect a visit from Family Services. I'll gladly help them pack your bags for the first foster home.

My sister's dirty nightgown fluttered out of the room. The smoke curled and sucked up behind her into the hall. I heard the bathtub run. There were three morning shows on her televisions. It was her job, she explained, to keep up with The Media.

I found a doughnut I'd forgotten in my jacket pocket. It had come loose from the napkin and the frosting smeared against the lining. I threw the jacket in the corner (an extra little treat to keep the spiders coming). I get too fat when I eat breakfast.

I found one of my sister's old coats in the hall closet. She has a terrible time parting with anything.

Just as Amanda began to scream, I unfastened the front door locks.

—Molly! Can you come here?! Please?!! I'm late for work!!!! MOLLY!!!!!

I couldn't fathom what would be worse: losing Mom or trying to survive Amanda. My sister's voice sailed with me all the way down the three flights, through the two downstairs doors of her apartment building, and out onto the street.

I had enough money to take the bus, or buy a dinner roll and Coke for lunch, or get this pair of blue sunglasses I'd seen that Friday in a secondhand store near the new school. I decided to use the money to call Amanda's boyfriend. Sometimes I like to imagine that in the last second I changed my mind and listened instead to the coins dropping through the phone right into the coin return; that I went to school that day with the sole purpose of buying those blue glasses. I've often wondered if my sister understood that there was something fated about my relationship with Nathaniel. I wonder if she had dreams about the way things would turn out with him.

The phone booth was gummy with someone's spilled

hot chocolate. I stuck and unstuck my shoes as I dialed. When Nathaniel's secretary asked who I was, I said an old friend from out of town.

She didn't like me or the idea of me, but she finally mumbled something and covered the phone. I heard her laugh with another woman, and then she rang me through.

I decided the best accent to use was French. I failed French three times, but my teacher always wondered how such a stupid girl could have such a flawless accent. I'm convinced all French teachers have bitter personalities. Probably because they had to leave France. I lit one of my sister's cigarettes and blew the smoke into the phone as if it was Nathaniel's ear.

—'Ello, I hope I don't catch you at a bad time, I said, letting my voice fill with the ambiance of Paris.

I could see him smiling at the other end of the line, charmed from the first. His office overlooked the choppy lake—and I was certain he stopped reading the papers on his desk and looked out at the mixed-up water.

—Who is this? he said in that mocking tone of his.

—I don't know how you say . . . it's about your motor scooter."

—Jesus. What . . . ?

—Oh, *non, ce n'est rien.* Everything's fine. It's just . . . this will sound impossible to you, I'm afraid. I've seen your 'Arley parked on Sutton. I guess we're neighbors. And a friend of mine works at the, uhn, how you say, Vehicles Department?

My sister's apartment was on Sutton.

—Department of Motor Vehicles, he said.

—*Mais oui.* And I asked her if she could get your name for me and then you were listed in the book of the phone and I felt particularly, how you say, *courageuse,* this morning.

I lifted one of my shoes again just to hear the sound of it unsticking from the moist chocolate. Across the street in the park, a man pushed a girl on a swing, fighting the breeze off the lake. Some acts, some images make life seem so normal, I thought.

—Yes? he laughed. It would be like him to find something amusing about a word like "courage."

—Well, I'm looking to purchase an . . . 'Arley and I really don't know anything about American motor scooters and you seem to have such a . . . sympathetic *figure,* face. This truly is silliness, I'm sorry, I should not have disturbed. . . .

Even then I knew that Nathaniel had anything but a sympathetic face. He said something but a semitruck went by and I had to shout: What?!

He wanted to know if some guy named David put me up to this. It took a while to convince him I was for real. Then he said: Look, could I call you back in a few minutes; something's come up here. What's your number?

I figured he'd try something clever like that. But I was prepared. I told him I was staying with this elderly couple, my sponsors, while I did modeling work in the States. I promised I wouldn't receive many phone calls at their place.

—But . . . perhaps you would let me buy you a cup of coff . . . an espresso for to bother you this way, I said.

—It would help to know your name, he said. He was such an easy man.

I had my thumb in *Beginner's French, Part Two,* and let it slide down the list of common female names.

—Yvonne, I said.

—Yvonne what?

Since I felt certain my troubles were seasonal in nature, I said: *Printemps.* Yvonne Printemps.

Then I lost my grip on the book and it hit the dead chocolate. I decided to leave it there for the next caller with a penchant for foreign languages. Meantime, I was sure Nathaniel put his shoes up on his desk and thought about the spring before he spoke again.

—Yvonne. Yvonne, he said, drifting for a while.

Drifting on the lake away from Amanda, where we all wanted to drift.

—You're a model, Yvonne?

Funny, but each time he said that name, Yvonne, it felt more possible to own it.

—*Oui,* uhn, lingerie, how you say, nightie gowns? Mostly for a French catalog.

—Yvonne . . . this is a practical joke. Right?

—No, no, no, I wouldn't. . . .

—What the . . . alright, he said, laughing at himself. He asked if I was familiar with a little hamburger place called Drummond's and suggested we meet at one o'clock the next day.

The line went dead, but the phone continued to hum, spiked with all that current. I kept the receiver pressed to my ear, hoping to be electrocuted by his scent, by any trace moisture that might have seeped through the phone from his voice. It seemed obvious at the time, that he didn't love my sister or he'd never agree to meet a lingerie hanger. (That's what my sister called models—hangers—because they cost her magazine too much money.) I thought it was pretty obvious he was just one of many to her. But if I had come right out and asked her, if I had told her I had a terrible thing for her boyfriend, she would have suddenly thought she wanted Nathaniel like lungs want air. She would have tormented him for a month or two with overboard passion until she got sick of the game of him; my sister had her ways. And so, I figured, why put him through all that?

I opened the phone-booth door and lit a fresh cigarette.

It wasn't that cold out. There were holes in the dirty ice clinging to the curb and I watched the melted snow rush toward the gutters. I used to dread the warm seasons because I was impossible then. I couldn't stay in and I couldn't sit still and I couldn't breathe and I couldn't eat.

I knew my sister would kick me out when the spring got serious. I thought she'd find some lost aunt who never had children and send me to her. I considered, however, that the aunt would turn out to be a pushover who lived by herself on an old farm. In time, I'd inherit all the money stashed under the floorboards of her farmhouse. Then I could go over to Paris and model nightie-gowns.

Or Nathaniel would take me in.

I was cracking myself up when my sister's car cursed its way toward the curb.

—Get in, she said, opening the door. But as soon as I

tried to, she made a pissy remark about the way the bottom edge of the door was scraping against the concrete and ice. So I backed up and said: I don't mind walking.

—Get in. Just pull up on the armrest.

I jimmied and played with the door and the amount of weight I put into the car so my sister's precious little roadster wouldn't suddenly roll over on its back, feet in the air, and die on her. I slammed the door and Amanda pulled into the stream of traffic heading downtown.

—I was calling to you before you left, didn't you hear me?

—No.

—Now I'm going to be even later. If you hear me screaming my head off, don't leave the house, okay? she said, honking at a sports car that wanted her lane.

—Okay.

—Here's fifty, is that enough?

I put the bills up to my nose, inhaling possibilities.

—This is for one week. *Alright?* Don't ask me for any more until Monday. Lunches, buses, and so on. *Alright?* Look, can I let you out here? I have to get on the Drive, she said, pulling over to the curb again.

—Jesus, I almost forgot. I set up a doctor's appointment for you. Here's the card, she said, drawing it from her wallet.

It read: DR. WILLIAM SANDERS, OB GYN, blah, blah, blah.

—That's today at four o'clock. Not next week. Or the week after. Today. He'll give you a prescription for the Pill. Just bring the prescription home. Edith can get it filled, okay? The thought of you getting pregnant is more than I can bear, she said. Her eyes began to swim again.

—Make sure and take the B train. God, whatever you do—she said to herself more than me—Don't take the A. I can just see you ending up on the West Side with some guy shoving a knife in your guts, and then you'll be in the hospital and Mom will be in the hospice and I'll be driving back and forth between the two of you all day, out of my mind.

I guess I didn't look sufficiently alerted.

—You have my number if anything happens to you. And Edith is there to help, okay?

I held the appointment card and said: But what if I'm still a virgin?

—That never lasts, she said in a cheerless way.

I hung on the door long enough to look at my sister. Amanda had a face Vermeer would have painted. She had a face shaped for ideal light, my mother liked to say. There was a sadness that had suckered every boy within reach since she was three years old—though she complained about the parts of her face as if she had a desperate need for reconstruction.

—I read that sperm can penetrate blue jeans, I said above the traffic noise.

—Just keep the appointment, she shouted. Then she leaned over, grabbed the door away from me and was gone.

I took a taxi to school that day and I really didn't mind that the driver kept getting lost along the way. You never know if it's intentional—that kind of getting lost—when you're suddenly driving down Chicago streets you've never even heard of, the meter out of control. But I cut the guy some slack, thinking maybe he was a foreigner or had a debilitating disease, or maybe he was an urban vampire dying at the wheel. Maybe the money he got from that one fare would support his family for a week, a day anyway. It didn't really matter in the end; the streets kept coming and I used the time to collect my thoughts. I would never understand my sister.

That pushy brain of hers was burning out like old paint cans and rags stored for the occasion.

I used to think the striking thing about Amanda was this intuitive stuff she had. Now I think we all have it, to one degree or another. Most of us try to keep it quiet because it isn't socially acceptable. Read enough *Ripley's Believe It or Not* and you realize most people are hiding something socially unacceptable. Or watch the news, or hang out anywhere really. You can see that people hide things in their faces. They'll let you see that much, that they're busy hiding something. And they always think those secrets make them more important than you, that it gives them some kind of godly power.

My sister hated her intuition because it was mostly about bad stuff. Nightmares that came true. So she tried staying up all night and she tried knocking herself out to avoid them. Sleeping pills, copious quantities of alcohol, light Chinese food before bed, heavy German breakfasts, bouts on the exercise bike, periods of lying on her bed like the Crucifixion but in a bloodless, groaning way from too much dark chocolate and coffee.

Her marriage was the worst.

She was nineteen and it lasted for all of six months. I was her only bridesmaid, so Amanda spent a ton on the clothes. She decided we were going to look like bored flappers with too much time on our hands. Something her fiancé Peter would find out too late. A Hungarian woman sewed thousands of dollars' worth of tiny colored beads onto our dresses. They crunched and chipped whenever I tried to sit on one of the dining chairs rented for the reception. I'm sure my sister was careful not to sit on anything hard or difficult the entire day.

The reception was held at our house, because Peter insisted on it, and he was footing the bill. My sister was so caught up in school—and the stellar career she intended from the first—she wasn't up for a fight. And then, as long as our mother was willing to do all the work. . . .

I was looking for the long, ivory cigarette holder my sister paid too much for down in Chinatown. One of my bridesmaid gifts. I had just started smoking, to get through the event. When I couldn't find it in my bedroom, I walked into Amanda's room. Too drunk to turn on the high light, I let things slowly take form in the dim glow from the closet. I rummaged through the overflow of wedding presents on her dressers, my fingers playing along the tissue paper of the open boxes.

—Take anything you want! Amanda's voice jumped at me from the dark. She was always sneaking up on me in that old house, jarring my heart. I realized she had been sitting on the edge of her bed the whole time.

—Sorry. I was looking for the cigarette holder.

—I think Peter was playing with it, she said.

Whenever I think of Peter I think of his broken nose. I believe she married him for his broken nose. She needed someone she could pull in close, who looked to the world the way she felt inside.

—Sit down, she said.

I sat next to her and listened to the party growing drunk and stupid in our mother's house. Amanda found a couple of cigarettes for us. There was something pleasant about smoking with my sister in those days, when she didn't talk about lung cancer or her responsibility to watch out for me.

—I had the worst dream in the world last night, she said, blowing her words into smoke rings that caught the closet light and disappeared.

—I don't want to hear it, I said.

—*She* was dead. . . .

I covered my ears.

When I thought Amanda was finished, I took my hands away.

She started in again.

—You wanted to bury her under the ballroom. We had these long crowbars. . . .

—You're worried because you're abandoning her, I interrupted.

—*No,* she said and looked at me as if I would never get anything right.

—She *died* and we *buried her* underneath the floorboards of the ballroom.

My sister enunciated every word as if the problem, all of life's problems, was my hearing.

—God, I hate it when you start psychologizing, she said.

—Every other week it's some new shitty nightmare, I said.

—Like it's my fault, she said, laughing at her dumb little sister.

—Mom's not going to die.

I grew quiet; determined that Amanda wouldn't get to me this time.

—Remember when I saw our grandfather's death? And when I knew that woman Dorothy was going to get into a car accident? And. . . .

She stopped, took the cigarette from my hand and stubbed it out next to her cigarette. Then she insisted on taking both of my hands in hers. There wasn't a thing I could do about it because it was her wedding day; I knew I had to try to be nice. And, if I struggled, the ashtray would dump over both our dresses.

—Look, Molly, what I'm trying to say is you'll never have to worry about someone being there for you as long as I'm around.

I slipped my hands away and reached over and blinded both of us when I turned on the bedside lamp.

—Are you on cocaine? I asked in all seriousness. I waited for her to open her eyes again so I could squint at her pupils.

—You sound like you're on cocaine.

—What do you know about cocaine, Imp?

—Probably more than you think.

I hadn't tried it, but a friend of mine had, in the bathroom at school. She told me it makes you larger than life—for a while. In any case, with my sister, even in those days, you had to sound like you knew everything; it was the only way she respected you.

She pushed her hip against mine, beads grinding against beads, to get me off her bed.

When I stood up, I think something occurred to her.

She said: I hope you aren't still worried about life being fair.

TWO

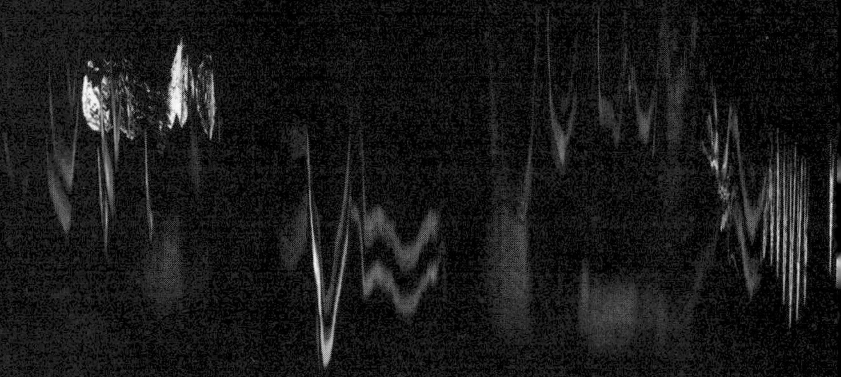

ALL GYNECOLOGISTS HAVE BIG KNUCKLES. That's what Sharon told me once, as she studied her own hands. She said being a gynecologist is how these guys get off. When they're doing it with their wives and girlfriends and mistresses, all they think about is doing it with their patients. So you have to keep an eye on them if they get a dreamy look or start reciting poetry or ask if you like sex or if you want to look at yourself in a mirror or anything that isn't straight exam. Even the women doctors, she said. Sharon didn't think there were any straight exams anymore because half the procedures were invented just to have some feel-good time.

She told me about the gynecologists that rape their patients and the ones that leave things inside, the ones that drug their patients and the ones that like to get their women aroused so slowly they hardly know how it all happened. And other things about bad operations and stirrups and cold equipment and stuff that Sharon was eager to tell me. But I was more interested in her ideas about modeling. I had to know what to say when I met Nathaniel.

There was something I liked about Sharon in those early days. When she got going you didn't really believe her but on the other hand you knew the things she said probably happened to somebody. She was a walking compendium of all the strange and creepy stuff that occurs out on the planet. And she was always generous about sharing her information, which is why she had few close friends and smoked too many cigarettes and cracked her knuckles incessantly.

When we were at lunch in the cafeteria, I told Sharon about this date I was going to have with an older man and that I had to come up with a disguise to completely alter my identity so he wouldn't recognize me. Sharon studied my face and laughed like I was planning to do something mean to a cat. Then she said we should skip school for the afternoon so she could help. Sharon loves anything of a sinister nature.

Her apartment was nearby, and she brought me home for the operation. I knew she had money, like most of the kids at the school. But I didn't realize just how much one can have and still be able to breathe. I was used to suffocating at the mere thought of money—the way Mom did each time the bills came. (I hadn't asked Amanda how she paid my tuition at that private school, but I suspected she suckered someone into a scholarship—Amanda had a way with people.) Sharon had spent the previous summer in Europe.

I wouldn't say she was that attractive, but there was something . . . it was hard to stop looking at her, even when you wanted to. She said everyone was sick of the beautiful thing—that I actually might think about modeling—if I had the right agent, and was willing to put up with the bullshit, and lost ten pounds. She explained about the camera adding weight. I might get some decent magazine work, a couple of good shows. I loved her authority; it came right out of a magazine.

Sharon threw herself on her soft, expensive bedclothes and stared at the ceiling. That's where she tried to retrieve her internal world—her one solace. It was easy to think of Sharon thirty years from now with children and husbands and houses, careers and projects and furniture—all strewn along the path of her life like so much litter, while she recuperated on her bed.

—This isn't about clothes, she said, getting up to open four closets, each the size of a tiny office. Each a suburb of the city of her apartment. She shook her head as if there was hardly a thing to wear.

—No? I said.

—No . . . this is about perception. It's a mind game. So, what kind of woman do you think this Nathaniel likes?

But I didn't have much to go on then. All I knew was that my sister and Nathaniel were the worst kind of match.

—Do you see him with someone . . . tall, short, bitchy, delicate, conservative, Bohemian . . . ?

—He rides a motorcycle, I suggested.

—And?

—And . . . I don't know.

While we talked, I was busy trying to count just the number of navy blouses in her closets. No other colors, no other shades of blue. I wanted to have one amazing fact to play with in my mind for a while. But Sharon interrupted my statistical analysis, demanding that I sit in one of her easy chairs and close my eyes.

I shut them as if I was sealing them with glue. It sounded like she sat down in one of the chairs across from me. I heard her breathe loudly. She told me to imagine Nathaniel in a restaurant, his date about to walk through the front door.

—Now see his date as she steps into the restaurant, starting with her shoes, Sharon said.

—Her shoes?

—Just do it.

Pretty soon, I was picturing myself lost in a shoe warehouse. Boxes of shoes up to the rafters. I was trying to pick the right pair.

—Let me know when you've got a clear image in your head, she said.

Few people had ever asked me, up until that point, what I thought about—I mean below the surface. And certainly not what I fantasized about. I did begin to see Nathaniel, fading in and out like a failing picture tube. Then I saw a parade of women cut from magazines, stepping out of movie screens. Sophisticated, airbrushed women. But Nathaniel seemed unhappy with them, irritated by the way the room turned to look at them. Or maybe he just didn't like their shoes—ill-fitting, clumsy shoes, every one of them.

My sister entered the restaurant wearing that fragile expression of hers. She pulled the door open, over and over again, and looked around the room for him. I wanted to see what kind of expression she'd make when she saw Nathaniel with his collection of perfect women.

Sharon interrupted.

—Would you say she's wearing high heels?

—I can't do this, I said, opening my eyes.

—Yes you can.

—What do *shoes* have to do with anything?

—It's this technique I read about. It's proven to work ninety-five percent of the time. Come on. Close your eyes and take a deep breath again, she said.

—Proven to work on what?

—On your . . . intuitive nature. Don't worry about it. Just try it.

I made a face, but tried again. I closed my eyes. We both breathed loudly into Sharon's room.

—There's a mysterious woman. Someone he's never met before. Someone you might not think, at first glance, would be his type. But she has this power over him. He comes completely undone when he's around her. All he can think about is how they're going to make it to the closest hotel, she said.

I hoped Sharon couldn't see the way my body began to fill with Nathaniel. I could picture him clearly. And the girl, who was me but not me, walked toward the crowd surrounding him. The women all looked alike.

Poised like cranes in the pond of my fantasy, they leaned on tall stools at skinny tables. My sister was perched on the tallest chair, and I realized that her hands were in fists; she was pulling on Nathaniel's jacket. Her face was bruised from crying. Maybe because he was dropping her but more likely because she'd grown tired of him. Tired of everything, tired of being tired of growing tired. She blamed him for making her feel that way.

I walked right up to all those same-faced women and pushed the ones in my way aside; I pushed aside the fatigue that hung like cigarette smoke. I got to where Nathaniel was trying to quiet my sister and I just shoved her off her stool. She grabbed at one of the high, narrow tables to steady herself. But that only brought the table down so it hit her in the temple as she fell. Before I could take a breath, I saw blood forming like a pillow under my sister's troubled head.

—I can't, I said, opening my eyes and getting up to pace the room.

—It works if you give it a chance, Sharon said, clearly annoyed with me.

We were both quiet. I went over and looked at a collection of china dolls I was sure no one had ever touched. Certainly they had never known the feeling of dirt on their shoulders or skirts, because the maid was always after them with a feather duster.

—My mother thinks they're cute, Sharon smirked.

Then she jumped to her feet and clapped her hands to get the attention of my unruly mind. She told me I would wear jeans, hand-tooled boots, a small T-shirt in bone, and a tailored jacket in lavender. It was imperative that I dye my hair platinum and wear contacts to change my eye color. She would pay for the salon appointment and a trip to her eye doctor. I'd have to miss school the next day, of course. She suggested I spend the night, because there was too much to do.

I walked over to the row of French doors that opened onto a balcony. Across the street the long park. Far reaches of lake and a good portion of the zoo. Some of the animals were in their outer cages now, with the start of spring. Amanda loved the zoo—a place where everything's safely contained, the worst behavior absolutely controlled. But I hated the zoo; still do. I feel the way the animals are trapped and overfed, walking in circles, knocking into bars.

—He'll know it's me, I said.

The whole thing was crazy.

—He might. But then it will be like a masked ball. You know who's trying to seduce you, but you pretend you don't, Sharon said. She opened up that giant smile of hers, that long-since-paid-for smile.

I didn't ask Sharon why she was doing all of this, but I thought I knew.

So I called to reschedule my doctor's appointment. While I was on hold, Sharon told me not to worry, she had enough rubbers to stitch together a Goodyear blimp. (Something her mother bought for her along with the stupid dolls.) I should fill my purse up before I left.

I called my sister's answering machine instead of talking to her secretary Edith. Edith was the world's biggest gossip. I said I was staying at a friend's. I didn't say which friend, in case my sister wanted to call and nag me about something. Sharon's mother agreed to call the school the next day to say I'd stayed over. She would say that Sharon and I both had the stomach flu. Sharon explained that as long as her mother had her teas and charities, parties and balls—and Sharon didn't publicly embarrass her—Sharon was pretty much left to her own devices.

I think the real thing about having money is that wealthy people make the world run at a different pace. Their teeth are set on edge by a different brand of adrenaline. Someone's always running to get them drinks and finger foods. Their cars go 200 miles an hour if they so much as look at the gas pedal. Doors open if they even think they want to go through them. Shop owners and businessmen drop everything for them—every last thing they need to do that day to avoid spontaneous combustion. The wealthy are "fit in" and get just what they want. And the little people who serve them talk very fast so the wealthy patrons don't have to listen to them very long. I think Sharon was addicted to that kind of speed.

After we got too little sleep that night—the sheets too comfortable, the bed too supportive, the maids too quiet in Sharon's apartment—the transformation took place.

We sped downtown and for hours people told me to shut my eyes so the hair trimmings and bleach solutions and hairspray wouldn't swim in them. They had to get the eyeliner on without permanently blinding me. I tried to adjust to the contact lenses. In between, I caught quick moments of Sharon making faces, pleased to death with herself.

When they were finished working me over, I stood up and looked in a full-length mirror. My eyes raced over this new, well . . . from the hand-tooled boots to the platinum hair . . . I couldn't even look into my own eyes for recognition. They shouted blue at me instead of muffled brown. Did I mention the shove-me-up bra?

I was suddenly ten years older, a model on her day off. Sharon was in heaven. She said I could come over and borrow clothes any time. There were several things she was planning to weed out of her closet anyway (her clothes did resemble vast fields of flowers, bountiful crops of color).

—I expect regular and detailed reports, Sharon said.

—Sure.

I didn't take her seriously; I didn't think it was possible to take Sharon seriously.

The valet got the car out of the lot and dropped me off across from the restaurant.

—You'll draw him in like flypaper, she said, purring in my ear. As a parting gesture, she gave me a hug and slipped a pair of sunglasses into my hands.

—They worked for Lolita, she said.

I didn't believe in her assessment that I had become something breathtaking.

—God, when he sees those headlight-blue eyes . . . , she said.

As soon as her car was out of sight, I turned to look in

a plate-glass window. I was standing in front of Saks Fifth Avenue. I wasn't lean enough, triumphant enough.

I went through Saks's revolving door and up to an idle woman at a makeup counter. Moving toward me, her fingertips skimmed the tops of bottles. She had this look like I was about to spend enough money to send her to the Cayman Islands for the rest of the season. When she got close, I saw that her smile had been applied in layers of product.

—Do you know what time it is? I asked.

I could see her heart fall a little through the center of her eyes. It's funny when you change your eye color. You're certain everyone else has changed their color too. I didn't believe for a minute her eyes were green. I was trying to find the subtle edges of her contacts when she told me it was one o'clock.

—Already? I said. I was too wound up to let myself think yet of Nathaniel across the street, opening a menu, checking his watch.

—Where do the days go? the woman laughed lightly.

—Would you recommend lavender shadow for my eyes? I said, fiddling with the samples on the counter. I didn't know if I had the nerve to meet him.

—You have such beautiful eyes, you could wear anything. I think I'd go with a color we call "aspiring violet," she said.

Suddenly I reached out and touched her perfectly manicured, gently-lotioned hand. And when I did, I realized that my hand was perfectly manicured and gently lotioned as well. It was like having a foreign object attached to my body.

—Would you believe I'm a model? I asked.

I saw this strange blush come over my skin-technician's face.

—Funny, but I assumed you *were* a model, she smiled and nudged a sample perfume bottle in my direction.

I picked it up and sprayed my neck, for Nathaniel.

—No, I mean would you think I was a model if you were going to make a bet with someone? I said.

—Well, you certainly *could* be a model, she smiled and reddened again.

She straightened the eye-shadow drawers in front of me. When she thought I had turned away, I saw her look over at one of the other idle salesclerks and roll her eyes; she couldn't wait to tell her about this one.

—But I mean . . . , I began, struggling to find the right way to get reassurance. I mean, what if I said I'd buy a thousand dollars' worth of makeup right on the spot if you could correctly guess whether or not I'm a model? I said.

My skin technician finally made a high, hissing sound like a valve being released.

—Maybe I could ask Mrs. Dixon to come over and join us—she was a model for several years, she said and gestured to her friend at the other counter.

My personal consultant repeated to Mrs. Dixon what I had said. Mrs. Dixon tried to keep a straight face. I sort of half-listened to their analysis because I was trying to spot Nathaniel in the window of the restaurant.

Before Mrs. Dixon could find something disingenuous to say to soothe my nerves, I said: Never mind, I'm late for an appointment.

As I left Saks, I was thinking about robbers and why so many of them wear disguises—a mask gives you steel, nerve.

The important thing to understand is that from the very first, I tried not to think about Nathaniel, the way an addict tries not to think about her drugs. I tried not to taste Nathaniel, the way someone baptized in chocolate will try to skirt the edges of a five-pound box of sweets. But the problem was, the winter snows were melting and running off the canopies of the handsome shops. The city salt trucks had all been parked in a giant lot for the year. And if I took that lavender jacket off I knew my nipples would harden but not freeze. There was no getting around the jumpy, insane spring when it came. Nathaniel was spring right up my thighs.

He was sitting at one of the back tables. I went over and introduced myself.

I couldn't tell if that twist of his lower lip meant he knew who I was or not. There were moments when I was sure Nathaniel knew my real identity, absolutely. Other moments I could see he didn't, without a doubt. That's the way it was with Nathaniel, there wasn't anything in-between about him, anything part-way or incomplete. He either knew or he didn't.

Perhaps I just seemed too old to be the person Amanda referred to as "the Imp" in that way she had of marking her territory.

—Yvonne, Nathaniel said, gesturing toward the seat across from him. He had this expression on his face that I wasn't sure about. All the blood and all the logical thought I owned rushed into the dead, white fibers of my hair.

—I'm so apologizing for being late, I said.

There was something—almost in the flesh—about sitting close like that that made me too conscious of my accent; I began to lose confidence.

—Nice perfume, he said.

He motioned to a waitress and returned to his drink. His second martini, an olive caught in the center.

—Saks Fifth Avenue, I said, as if this was the name of a perfume—the fragrance of the self-assured, the confident, the justifiably aloof. I began to watch his mouth, his lips, losing myself there.

Nathaniel laughed and without really taking his eyes off me, he opened his menu. But he knew it by heart, so he closed it again and looked down at the floor as if he had dropped something. He drained his glass.

I should have asked those women over at Saks if I had model's legs; that was the real question. I should never have agreed to meet at Drummond's. I knew Nathaniel and Amanda ate there together all the time. I kept imagining her walking through the door. That fragile look before she came undone. I'm certain now that he wanted her to catch him, or us. Even if he knew she'd be somewhere else that afternoon, he must have imagined that a friend or a busboy would spot us and report back to my sister.

Our waitress didn't write anything down when we gave our orders. She was the kind who can stack the entire North Side up one arm, while carrying several coffeepots in the other. It was obvious that she knew Nathaniel. While they chatted, she gave me the same kind of look he was giving me. He ordered another martini.

Beneath his unshaven face was an impression left by everything in his life that had gone wrong for Nathaniel when it should have gone well, as though he had lost his grip along the way. I don't mean money and enterprise, but I think he just didn't care to hold onto things the rest of us hold close.

As soon as the waitress left, I began this nonsensical talk about motorcycles. Something about my parents forbidding me to ride them as a teenager. Now that I was independent, I was determined to do as I pleased. As I stuffed immense bites of hamburger in my mouth and took deep inhalations of Coca-Cola, I continued to build on my story. I didn't give Nathaniel a chance to interrupt, but I think he was satisfied to watch me squirm.

Eventually, he reached over and took hold of my arm. His grip made it possible for me to shut up. Then he smiled at my sunglasses.

—You aren't French. Are you?

My father, the inscrutable psychologist, was a ruthless game player. A master strategist. And a cheat, if the whole truth ever comes out. He told me that in any game worth playing, especially a good mind-game, you have to know when to let the other player take a pawn, or get an answer, or pass through a section of a maze they've been trapped in for too long. Otherwise you run the risk of being trapped there yourself, of losing the whole thing and hating yourself in a foolish way.

My father was no comfort to me when I knew him, but a few of his bitter comments on life stuck. I've used them like a small bottle of painkillers for which there is no refill.

I looked at Nathaniel's mouth again and I leaned forward as if I was going to kiss him. He waited for that kiss. But I pulled back and laughed in a silly way. I bit one of my nails. The polish was still a little soft and I left my teeth marks there. I sipped my Coca-Cola and said in my flat, Midwestern way: No, I'm really not.

He watched me pucker my lips as if I could pull the right conversation from the tip of the air.

—So we're even, I said.

—Even? He turned the medicine inside his glass and knocked it back.

Then he took four extra-strength aspirin from a tin he carried in his jacket and swallowed them without so much as a drop of water. He ordered another drink and tried to get me to order one. But I was thinking about the dessert tray. Sharon told me models are notorious for eating junk, which was a good thing because I felt ravenous.

—Would you like dessert, he smiled.

—If you would, I said. I hoped I sounded coy.

—Sure.

We split the last piece of Black Forest cake.

—So, you say we're even?

—Well . . . I began, my mouth full of cake. You knew I wasn't French from the beginning, but you pretended you believed me, I said.

It was a wild guess, to suggest he knew all along. An idle cat-and-mouse affair, but I was right.

—Your accent is pretty bad, he said.

—I'd like another piece of cake, I said.

—Am I making you hungry?

—Mmm.

—Mmm, he said, as he leaned forward and touched one of my legs, just above the knee.

I didn't mean to jump. And I felt so ridiculous I didn't even notice I'd knocked my quiet little purse off the table at first. Following that smile of Nathaniel's down to the floor, I saw all the condoms. They were scattered about as if they'd just burst from a confetti egg. Happy, trouble-free colors spilled at his feet. The ones with ribs and flippers and rings; the ones with tiny photos of cheesy-looking couples lost in each other at the beach; the ones that promised to taste like TV dinners and frozen yogurt; the ones that smelled like sheep or lost little lambs.

I wanted to laugh as easily as Nathaniel. But I was trying to figure out which was going to draw more attention. Should I leave them until the waitress stepped in them or should I scoop them back into my purse while the suddenly-curious neighbors looked on?

I don't know if Nathaniel would have been considered a gentleman. Or what that means, or who cares. It's one of those words that's too old and full of disappointment to even matter. In any case, he quickly pushed those wrapped invitations back into my bag, which he handed me under the table. He put money down by one of his empty glasses and took my hand. We went out to the street together like we were a couple in a great hurry. I thought we were. The sun greeted us at such an angle when we first stepped outside, that we were blinded for a moment, at least I was. Struck blind, in great need of a taxi. I knew everything was happening because the snow was melting and because the spring wouldn't leave me alone.

Sharon told me that morning—while the stylists were stripping my hair of all its God-given color and munching on my cuticles like locusts—that if you watch a man closely you'll discover where his greatest weakness lies. If he goes for your ears first, she said, he's guaranteed to fall apart if you so much as whisper in his. If he can't wait to run the tip of his tongue against the roof of your mouth, he'll start throbbing in his pants if you do it to him. Nathaniel, I would later report, was a man who goes for the throat.

We had gone two or three blocks in a yellow cab when Nathaniel told the driver to "keep his eyes on the road." I felt certain, in that moment, that life is a constant rerun of an old movie. The driver nodded or winked or smiled. I'm not sure, it happened so fast in a blur of skyline and traffic and bridges and river. Nathaniel's scent was a strong alcohol that melted me from chin to collarbone. I kept trying to catch my breath and felt crazy dizzy. I was pulled down into the taxi as if I was helping Nathaniel to drown. I started kissing and licking his neck like he was spring on a stick.

He turned me around so my back was to him, in that strange way he had of getting close. He couldn't see what was moving across my face, but I'm certain he could intuit it. With great care he unzipped my jeans and pulled them down around Sharon's hand-tooled boots. There was nowhere to look except at the vinyl of the seat where I was pressed or out at the horizon of people. Mostly their heads.

They rushed through the streets as if they all had to find someone to tell that I was doing it with my sister's boyfriend in a yellow cab.

He moved a hand over my bottom and up between my legs. Then nothing. I waited, sick with love—thousands and millions of faces went by, in and out like strange reception. Nathaniel withdrew his hands and the cab stopped at a light. Maybe having me didn't matter nearly as much as knowing that he could.

I pulled my jeans up and turned to look at him. He was shaking his head, smiling to himself. Not maliciously but like a guy who's won a serious bet on the horses or football or something.

The cab began to move again and I was looking for a Kleenex. I was all worked up. Nathaniel smiled at me, and gave me a kiss on the cheek. He took out a card and penciled a number on it.

—You better think about what you're doing before you use this, he said.

I was to call him at that number instead of the office. He gave the driver a couple of twenties and told him to take me where I wanted to go.

Nathaniel slammed the cab door so it fit snug, without a lot of noise, and the cab pulled away. I turned and looked out the back window. He was crossing the street, and I think he was going to hail another taxi.

I still couldn't tell if he knew it was me or not.

THREE

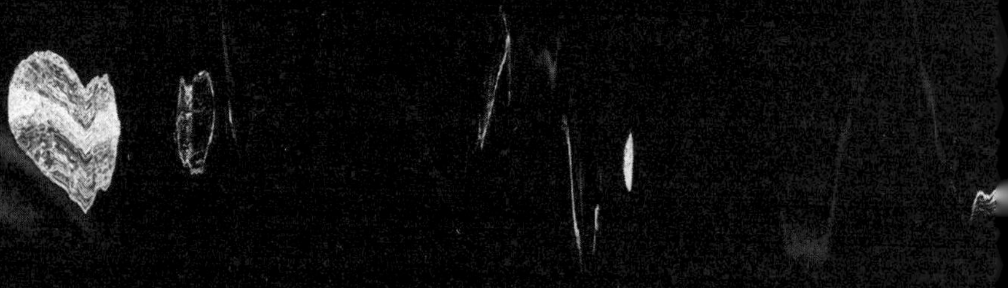

THE TAXI DROPPED ME BY THE LAKE, CLOSE TO MY sister's apartment. Along the concrete bank were gang hieroglyphs, one long canvas against the world. The wind had come up so the only people around were sitting in their cars in the parking lot. I had to climb a fence to get down to the beach and I managed to tear a hole in Sharon's jacket. When the wind yowled I didn't resist; I let it push me to the end of the sand and then right into the water. Once I was out there, I actually thought I saw the waves turn direction.

I was looking for something out in the horizon that day—some kind of vision painted out there that would tell me what to do. Not about sleeping with Nathaniel. It was the rest. But all I could see at that moment were the things churned up, the paper and cellophane and scum moving in the water. A freezing stew of memory, dead fish. I considered standing there for the rest of my life. I knew about the undertow, but I was surprised to find out just how strong it was. I had to fight my way back to the beach.

Exhausted, I dropped onto the sand. It wasn't that I wanted to wash Nathaniel out. I'd never want that. It was something else.

From the minute Nathaniel got out of that cab, I had begun to think about Mr. Graf, the boarder my family took in one year, and by the time I had gotten to the beach, I was in a state. This wasn't the first time. Mr. Graf was a vicious little memory in constant need of a burial. The problem was, I didn't know where to dig without hitting his skeleton, uprooting his bones. But that doesn't explain it.

Years ago, our father, the noted psychologist and unbearable tyrant, left. Once the attention around his abrupt departure died down, my mother suddenly had to manage a financial picture that read like a foreign language she couldn't identify. The concept of capital gains was her personal demon through those first months of restless nights. I remember her wandering in a terrified state down to the kitchen she could no longer afford.

Finally, on the bad advice of trusted friends, which oozed into the dry rot of our fortunes, my mother sold the house where my sister and I had grown up, and purchased a once-grand home in a nearly abandoned neighborhood. It wasn't far from one of the worst areas of the lakeside, but her friends felt certain it was on its way to urban renewal. She called it Wharton Manor.

It was the kind of place that had skeleton keys. There were seven bedrooms, three maid's rooms, a massive kitchen with pantries inside pantries, a dining room, living room, library, sitting room—and a ballroom with long mirrors and windows of original glass, which my mother loved to touch like a collection of old, familiar bottles. Wharton Manor came complete with a working buzzer system to call the ghosts of maids past. Buttons I liked to push frequently, since the harsh rasping sounds wrecked my sister's nerves.

We managed to clean and furnish a small portion of the living room, part of the kitchen, and a bedroom for each of us. The stately garden with its large fountain was too overgrown, too thorny for us ever to tackle, the waterworks jammed up years ago. The rest went the way of the hope for urban renewal.

My mother purchased long and unfriendly relationships with building contractors, an unending string of frightening utility bills, and a daughter who grew to hate what all that stone and mortar did to her social life. Amanda wouldn't invite a soul to the house, and to fully express her bitterness, she refused to take public transportation, making our mother drive her everywhere. This, in turn, crippled Mom's efforts to line up full-time work.

But I had a sense about the house that I was unwilling to surrender to Amanda's bad humor, or my mother's way of quietly drowning off by herself in the middle of the night in the pantry, or to the terrible event of our boarder, Mr. Graf.

It must have been the summer before my sister's senior year. Amanda pulled me aside and said we had to have an urgent meeting in the garden after supper. Hidden in the ruins was a small building nearly choked off by ivy. This became Amanda's studio where she sketched, and wrote, and thought too much. It might have been a gardener's shed once, but there was no evidence of any earthly labors there. From somewhere Amanda had acquired an Oriental rug, a table, and a couple of chairs.

It was, my mother and I were made to understand, Amanda's private sanctuary; we weren't allowed to go inside unless we had Amanda's express permission. And then only when she was present to accompany us.

That night she actually let me look around and sit in the more comfortable of the two uncomfortable chairs. She narrowed her eyes into sharp objects aimed toward the kitchen windows. I could see our mother inside, laboring over the sink.

—I'm suffocating in that house, aren't you? Aren't you suffocating? she asked.

The concept of being unable to breathe in a house the size of a small government building—which was so drafty no one ever felt truly warm the entire winter—was something I needed time to consider. But my sister hated it when I mulled over questions not intended for mulling. She snapped at the air as if I was a circus flea who hadn't performed on cue.

—WE ARE DYING IN THAT HOUSE, she said.

I felt a drop from her poisonous tongue fly into my face and burn my cheek. You can't breathe, you can't eat, you can't think in such a house. And if those were the only problems, I could lead a blissful life, she grinned. You must realize how it's gobbling up our futures—as we sit here. Gobbling them up! My future and your future and, God knows, *her* future, she said.

Amanda often referred to our mother in the third person. But then Amanda had become angry with her from the second our father left. She had never tried to hide it. It was as if our mother had something to do with his disappearance or could have prevented it or should have at least been able to find him.

—Do you know what I saw on her dresser today? Do you have any idea?

She was heating up and I could smell the bug repellent she had slathered on her body.

—No, I said, conscious of holding my breath.

—Of course you don't. Because you think you can just screw around and nothing matters. Not a blessed thing. You can hang out with your friends all day, do as you please. You could steal, cheat, lie and who would know the difference? Because *you're* the innocent. But I try and do one thing, just one thing constructive for this family, and everyone jumps on me. Never mind that I'm sacrificing my life here—just never fucking mind.

She stopped her tirade and studied me. I watched her face shift. She took a package of cupcakes off her writing table and tossed it to me.

—I'm just trying to take care of you, Imp; I didn't intend to say it in a mean way. Of course you want to run around and play. God knows, I did at your age. But what's going to happen when you want to go to college?

It had never occurred to me that anything would happen when I wanted to go to college; I'd just go. Everyone expected me to go. I split the first cupcake apart and licked the white center.

—And what in God's name is going to happen to *me?* It's just a little over a year away, she threatened.

I didn't understand what would go wrong with my sister's future either, but I felt like I was trying to push the cupcake into the place where the worst possibilities wanted to lodge.

—The point is, I mean the entire point here is that there won't be any MONEY for me to go to college. Even if I go to the stinking junior college downtown. Because what I saw on her desk last week was a bill to fix the furnace. And do you have any idea how much that bill was for?

—A hundred dollars? I asked, getting to the next white center where I wished I could fall in, like falling into a cloud, changing shape, blowing far away, far apart.

—God, to be young again. Try three THOUSAND dollars.

—Come on, I laughed, the mouthful of cupcake sticking in my throat.

—Come on, fuck! she said, hitting the arm of her chair. She got up and paced.

—Three THOUSAND dollars, she said, coming over and petting my hair as if she had to calm *me* down.

—I've been up for days trying to figure out how we're going to save this wretched situation. How to save *you.* I'm sure you've noticed the circles under my eyes. I couldn't go to school today because my eyes looked so bad.

Her eyes looked no different than they always did to me. The same violet eye shadow and black eyeliner, the mascara and curled eyelashes—fifteen counts with the eyelash curler on each eye. I used to watch her till she'd push me away, saying I was taking up her personal air.

—A couple of days ago, I came up with a plan. But it won't work without your help. So if you can't help, you better tell me now and we can just burn the whole fucking place to the ground. Then we can go on welfare and live like a pack of starving rats, she said.

I used to think my sister was serious about everything she said before I understood about dramatic personalities. Amanda had a way of enlisting my help—of making me stick a broken thumb in a twenty-story dam before I knew the assignment. Then, often enough, she'd walk away, leaving me to sort things out.

To prevent a long session in her musty little studio, I said: Alright.

—Since she's incapable of getting a full-time job and we have little left in the way of savings, the only thing we can possibly do is rent out rooms.

—Boarders?! Mother would never take in boarders, I assured her.

—Of course she wouldn't. She doesn't have a creative fold in her entire brain.

—I don't. . . .

—Never mind. Look, there are only so many choices here. And I don't think any of us are becoming hookers, Amanda said.

The hot air froze around my ears and I was suddenly aware of mosquitoes—the ones that bred in the old fountain and nested in my sister's Oriental rug, the ones that rushed from the lake in great clouds on long summer evenings.

I began to smack my legs and neck and arms while Amanda made the whole thing absolutely simple for my simple mind. She spoke loud enough for me to absorb her words above the sound of the mosquitoes.

She explained that Mom had ruined everything by buying such a big house, but at least there were rooms to rent out to several boarders. A few quiet renters were the only solution to such a dire situation, Amanda explained. My sister had, it seemed, met the perfect individual to be the first renter; he could take one of the maid's rooms way in the back of the house. His name was Mr. Graf. He was a man who had few belongings, who would hardly breathe when he was there, and who didn't like to eat meals with families or interfere in other people's lives in any way. He would probably be taking frequent trips.

I tried to imagine how my sister might have met such a person. It couldn't have been at school. But I thought that was my sister's whole life—her entire social life—school. I didn't realize that, with only a year left, that world had worn thin as an old uniform; she spent as little time there as possible.

—I hope you realize the trust I'm investing in you. Because this has to be a mutual decision—we have to convince her together that this is the only way.

—I don't know. I think Mom's having a hard time right now, I finally said.

—When isn't she having a hard time? Look, the room's so far away it might as well be in another country. And this person is really quiet. So, do I have your word on this?

—I don't know, I said.

—Look, this is for you! she screamed.

—Alright, as long as this boarder doesn't upset Mom, I said.

I went to bed early that night, after taking a bath in baking soda and dabbing alcohol on all of my bites. I didn't want to look at my mother's face when my sister brought up the idea of boarders again.

Amanda showed me once how to put an empty drinking glass against a wall in order to hear the loudest parts of a conversation going on in an adjoining room. So while the summer heat rolled through the house and pressed down from the empty attic above, I worked on listening to my sister pitch her idea to our mother.

I heard the word "no," and then I heard "No," and then "NO" again. Then it got quiet for a while. I knew my sister was sucking up all the spare heat left in the city—all the reserves stored in the earth and in the concrete and steel—drawing them into her lungs to give her voice the strength it needed.

I put the glass down and listened, lights out, pretending to sleep in case anyone wanted to drag me out of bed to settle something. After a horrible wait, it started. She called my mother weak and insensitive, useless and fat. She said my mother would never have another boyfriend, another chance at life. She was too old to have a good career, too impotent to handle her financial affairs. "This stupid house" of hers was my sister's proof of everything that was wrong with my mother.

I knew Mom felt too sad or lost or hurt to answer. So Amanda kept going. She said her clothes were out of style, her eyeglasses a public embarrassment, her car uglier than a hearse. She rode my mother for being born with dark facial hair—though I knew the constant efforts my mother made with bleach and tweezers and wax.

It was in the nature of my sister's episodes to throw anything at hand into the pot. Amanda was ruthless, thorough, and loud, her great spoon stirring us into a state until she was so exhausted, so drained, all she could do was break down and cry.

It was that long, building moan that crippled us. The sound Amanda made when she threw herself against her own burning rocks. When it reached a pitch that no one should have to bear, we would do anything to rush to comfort her, to quiet her, to assure her things would be all right. We pled with her to stop crying; we asked to be forgiven. We told her we just wanted her to be happy.

When I finally got out of bed, I did my best to miss the more restless floorboards in the hall. Then I stood by the crack of my mother's bedroom door. I saw Amanda in her arms, both of them rocking back and forth, as if there had been a drowning—and no one knew who had gone under, who had been rescued.

Mr. Graf moved in a week later. We were not, Amanda explained, to seek him out or trouble him in any way under any circumstances. Unless, of course, there was a fire He was a man, she said, who had experienced a tragic loss in recent years and wished to remain alone and undisturbed. Although Amanda thought at first that he would only take one room, she was pleased to announce he would be renting all three of the maid's rooms, using the tiny kitchen that came with those quarters. Thanks to the arrangements with Mr. Graf, not only would we keep the house, she beamed, she and I would attend good schools.

We had that talk over breakfast, at Amanda's insistence—though we rarely ate a single meal together—and Mother was brave enough to ask where Amanda had met this fellow.

Amanda said it was a funny turn of events. At the public library she ran into one of Dad's old colleagues, Dr. Haymer, and they got to talking. Amanda told him about our empty old house and Dr. Haymer said he happened to be looking for a place for a dear friend and so on. While they were settling that business, I stared into my full bowl of cereal, not really hungry. My thoughts were quickly lost when Amanda jumped up and said she had to get ready for school. I knew she'd only answer one question about our tenant, if that, so I tried to pick carefully. But in my hurry, all I could say was: What does he do?

—What? she said, as if everything had been finalized and there was nothing more to discuss.

—What kind of job does Mr. Graf have? I tried again.

Like the monarch who suddenly decides, purely on a whim, to grant a benevolent wish to one of her nameless eunuchs, Amanda smiled at me for a long while.

—He's a hypnotist. A retired hypnotist, she said.

FOUR

I'M NOT SURE WHAT I EXPECTED FROM DEATH that year. It certainly wasn't my mother, despite my sister's premonitions.

A couple of days after I'd been with Nathaniel in the taxi, my sister took me out to see Mom. Amanda was pissed at me the whole way and wouldn't say why. She did tell me this might be the last visit, because our mother had gotten so bad. But when I first saw Mom looking pleased to see us, practically glowing, I was sure Amanda said that so she wouldn't have to drive me out to see her anymore.

Mom insisted we meet in a park along the North Shore, not far from the hospice. Amanda said Mom didn't want me, in particular, to see her in bed "like that." Dying of cancer, and she got up and took a goddamn taxi to sit in a public park to see her kids. I had whole nights of seeing "like that" play on the ceiling above my bed.

Mom was badly winded, but then she had been that way for some time. Her skin was the same pale wallpaper color, and her hair was growing back though it felt like down. She hadn't lost much weight that I could tell, but she had that kind of invisible weight; you wouldn't necessarily know if she'd lost twenty pounds.

Amanda wanted some time alone with her. So I had to sit on a bench on the other side of the park and look busy. I didn't understand why we had to meet with her separately, as if my sister and I were taking turns in a confessional, but I knew everyone was exhausted from trying to play family at that point. At least they didn't get into a fight. I credit Mom with that. Before long, Amanda got up and took off in her car. I suspected she went to find a place with plenty of magazines, maybe a phone to call Nathaniel.

I came over and sat down on the bench next to Mom, wondering what to say. She smiled at me for a long time. The trees were crowded in around us like people you can't shake. It would have been easier if we'd had a vista to focus on. But the North Shore guards its property well—and the great views are intended for those who can pay for them. As it was, I spent too much thought on the muumuu my mother wore and the winter coat that didn't close all the way. I assumed the pink stains down the front were medicine. She held a brittle plastic box on her lap, yellowed with age. Mom had a thing about putting everything, her entire life, in plastic boxes. As if each see-through enclosure would make her more secure, more tranquil, able to cope.

We waited for an elderly couple to pass before we said anything. They smelled of old money and dry cleaning and were dressed in plaid, tailored outfits. The kind of people who express scorn for all the impoverished people of the Earth. The miniature poodle in tow, suffering under their anal-retentive watch. All three of them looked at my mother as if she was a bag lady, I an ex-con.

Mom tilted her head and smiled like she finally recognized someone in a photograph.

—You're wearing a wig, she said.

—Mmm, I said, tired of its sweaty, close feel.

—Why?

—So Amanda doesn't give me grief about dying my hair.

—Oh. You dyed your hair?

—It was just a thing to do, I said.

—Of course.

That was my mother. If I told her I was about to serve ten years in a state prison for some heinous crime, she'd simply say: "Of course."

—Would you like *my* wig? she said with sudden enthusiasm. It was as if she'd found something to please me.

—I haven't worn it much. They're itchy when you don't have any hair. I could . . . mail it to you, she beamed.

—I'll think about it, okay?

—I have some things for you, Mom said, trying to coax the lid off her plastic box.

—You look well, I said, still harboring the hope that she was faking her illness.

—They're taking very good care of me.

She smiled timidly and patted my hand in a grand-mother way, which was her way.

—I mean you don't even look sick, I insisted. Then I realized what was in her box.

—Thank you, sweetheart.

—What does the doctor say about the tumor?

My mother seemed surprised, as if someone, my sister in particular, should have told me.

—I don't see the doctor anymore.

She set the box down by her side on the hard-packed soil of a flowerbed; she had no other place. When she moved I realized my mother wasn't wearing the perfume she always wore. Imagine returning to a garden that you haven't seen for a while, and it's late April, and you suddenly realize that nothing, not one single plant or herb or flower around you has any smell at all. That's what it was like.

—Why?

—Because I've stopped the chemo, she said.

—Thank God, I said before I could catch myself. All I could think about at first were the times I'd seen her after a treatment.

—There's a cluster of tumors now. . . . But look, I want to show you what I brought, before . . . I made such a fuss with the taxi driver that he get here on time; he'll kill me if I'm not sitting by the gate at one, she said.

While my mother opened the first of several jewelry boxes, a wedding party pulled up in limos and began to gather on the high slope of the grass, not far from our bench, to take photographs. It seemed we had picked a place that had the advantage of particularly good light. There were more bridesmaids than I cared to count, and flower girls, and ring bearers, and a sickening amount of hope and money spent.

I didn't want Mom to be asked to move, because I could see myself doing something violent if they did. At the same time, I didn't want her to show up in the background of one of their sickening pictures. We watched them for a while, and neither of us talked of moving. The bridesmaids swarmed like restless bees over the lawn, puncturing the ground with their stinger heels. They wore narrow dresses in deep purple, but my mother said: How strange, to pick black for a bridesmaid color.

I figured her eyesight was affected by the morphine. She was experiencing the wedding party as a death wedding, a funeral wedding in black, an event put on for her surreal morphine benefit. I didn't correct her, thinking I would only make her feel bad. But later I wished I'd said something.

When I finally looked down at my mother's hands, I saw she was holding a papier-mâché pin I made for her in grammar school. Part of it broken off, the poster paints dull and worn.

She was giving it back to me.

In fact, the box was filled with the odd things I had given her over the years. She was returning them all to me.

I guess she didn't know what else to do with them. The pearl earrings I gave her for her last birthday, the silk scarf from Christmas.

I did everything I could to choke off my tears.

—Isn't there anyone else I can live with? I asked.

My mother's eyes reddened.

—*Anyone* else? I pleaded.

—Another year and you'll be off at college. Look, does this fit you? she said in her gentle, ignoring way. She pulled a ring with a large moonstone out of the box. Because if it doesn't, it's just silver and you can't really have it fitted.

That's when I finally lost it. I leaned my head into my mother's chest, the great couch of her arm. And as the tears ran, I watched everything in the plastic box blur and wash away. I could see it all being swept from her lap; lost things that could sink to the bottom of the lake without any trouble.

When I was finished, I sat very still. I suddenly recognized the smell that used to reside underneath her perfume. I wondered if I'd be able to remember that particular smell at will, or if the perfume she started wearing after her illness would be all I had left. As soon as I pulled myself together, my mother began to fiddle with that box again. She had everything spread out on both her thighs, trying not to drop anything. She wanted to show me that the bottom was filled with empty wooden spools.

—I've had these for years, she said.

She took one of them up, and her hands were shaking; she tried to thread a shoelace into it, but couldn't.

—Well, you'll figure it out. You just string them together

like a necklace. No one makes wooden spools anymore. It will be something to remind you of me . . . when my grandchildren are playing.

When I said nothing, she added: Your children can play with them, see?

As if I didn't understand what she was talking about the first time. I avoided telling her I wouldn't have children, that there are abortions for things like that. Then we heard the taxi, and my mother was supposed to leave. But when she got up, just the exertion of walking a few steps—she could hardly breathe, and you could see she was in pain and she wouldn't let anyone help her.

We were both crying. The taxi driver was crying, I think.

When she was finally sitting in the cab, the door propped open, she turned to me, and caught as much of her breath as she could.

—Look, those bridesmaids' dresses are purple, not black. Isn't that funny? she said with relief.

She kissed me lightly on the cheek and told the driver to go.

Amanda made me sit there a whole hour before she came back to the park. I was too burned to talk with her by then and she was in some kind of mood, too. I imagined she'd spent the whole time on the phone with Nathaniel. Maybe the subject of platinum hair and dark wigs came up. Or maybe he just told her, "I think I almost did your baby sister the other day." In either case, there wasn't anything I could do about it just then.

My sister took the scenic route—as if we had some need for scenery—past the old mansions along the shore, their tennis courts, high iron gates, lawns like golf courses, things in bloom defying the weather. That was her vision of success—living in one of those dead places. But Amanda would spend her entire life hoping to arrive even if she got there. The dog chasing its tail and all that.

—Don't you get it? You may never see her again, Amanda said in a low, boiling tone.

—You said that.

I put my bare feet up on the dash and looked away. I felt like telling her about my luncheon date.

—I can't believe you wore a wig.

—You noticed, I said.

—Why not wear a hospital gown and stick hypodermic needles in your arms?

I turned to consider my sister's tragic face and said: You thought I was making fun of her?

—I suppose you weren't.

—You're sick, I said.

For a long while the silence of those big, empty-looking houses tried to fill my sister's car.

—Alright. Why then? Why did you wear a wig?

I wanted to tell her about Nathaniel, but I knew it was something I should hold in reserve for a while. There would be a better moment.

So I gave her my ready answer about a failed experiment with hair dye, and how a friend at school had loaned me a wig of hers until I could figure out what to do about it.

I assumed Amanda would try to pull the wig off and we'd end up swerving all over the road in a big fight and get into a car crash and die on the way back from seeing our dying mother and then no one would have to worry about anyone anymore. But she just laughed.

She turned the news on the radio way up and quickly forgot about me—and a whole lot of things, I guess.

Curled into the leather of my sister's car, I hoped to sleep for a while, but the old wound of Mr. Graf had no intention of healing up, now that it had been reopened.

Early on, I had a curiosity about him that seemed to run on alternating currents. I had the impression that he was an elderly man. I probably had the word "retired" confused with age, and I wasn't very interested in old people then. I was at that time of life when you do desperate things to get out of an afternoon visit from a great-aunt or a grandparent. They made me too restless, too crazy.

It was only when I began to tell a friend about renting out rooms in our house, or when I heard a noise coming from the maids' quarters, or when it suddenly occurred to me in the middle of the night that my sister had probably invited a serial killer to stay in the bleak rooms at the back of the house, that I reminded myself to find out about Mr. Graf.

I wondered if this hypnotist thing was just something for Amanda to say. Our father had hated hypnotists. He had, in fact, written a couple of psychology papers on the subject. He also had no patience with faith healers, astrologers, and magicians—people he boxed into the same general category.

A week after Mr. Graf moved in, I realized I hadn't seen him come or go even once. Not to stroll, or stretch, or piss in the bushes. He seemed to be without a car—we knew all the cars parked near the house—and I never saw him run for a bus. If he came or went, it must have been when Amanda and I were off at school and my mother was busy struggling with her miserable part-time jobs. Maybe when she made her desperate runs for groceries and supplies.

There were times when I was tempted to push into his side of the house, like a baby pushing her head against a necessary membrane. In my travels through the manor, I had found an entire set of skeleton keys. They were tucked away in a nook off the second pantry along with a silver rattle, a bone thimble, and a small cloth doll. This might have been one of my sister's stashes, but my suspicion was that the objects were hidden away by a maid or a small child who had lived in the house.

I heard Mr. Graf moving about at various hours of the day or night. He made scraping noises that ran through the house striking at raw nerves, and tapping sounds so faint I had to put my ear to the floor to make sure I wasn't imagining them. Water ran for what seemed like hours.

I remember sitting at the kitchen table, which was one of the few places for things that needed to float on an island above the floor; we had little in the way of furniture. I was trying to build something for a science project out of toothpicks, Elmer's glue, and an old pack of playing cards my father had left behind, all the while cursing the existence of science and my teachers for thinking it could do something for my life, cursing my father for using such slick cards, when my mother suddenly decided in one of her whimsical moments to bake Christmas cookies for everyone she'd ever met.

It was only September, but she wanted to try out the arsenal of cookie cutters she'd found for a song at the Salvation Army. Gearing up, I guess, because she hated the holidays and was known to spend hours, sometimes days, buried in her room trying to ignore their passage. She often left my sister and me to wander over to the greasy spoon a few blocks down for our holiday meals. Sometimes we went our separate ways, sometimes as orphans fed by other people's parents.

Of course my fragile structure toppled the minute Amanda walked into the kitchen. I looked up to see a vision of hair rollers and pink lipstick scowling at me.

—I told you I've got a final tomorrow, she said, pouring herself a glass of water as loudly as she could.

Usually she'd do anything to avoid our company, and had glasses and bowls and spoons and cereal boxes and peanut butter—a small pantry in her bathroom so she wouldn't have to come downstairs when we were at home.

—So? I said.

—I'm not talking to you, midget.

—I know you'll do well; you always do well, Mom said while rolling out a cool sheet of prospective cookies next to my rubble of cards. I watched the way a couple of the toothpicks were inadvertently swept up into her dough, and how she simply ignored them and kept going.

—Fine. But who can concentrate when the entire house smells like . . . God, Mother, what are you doing?! Amanda said.

It had taken my sister a minute to realize that every bit of counter space, the top of the fridge and the radiators, all of the kitchen chairs and the appliances were filled with cooling racks and cookie sheets and plates of cookies.

—They're all deformed! Amanda howled.

—I found this marvelous recipe book at the library, Mom started in, paying no mind to my sister's comment. Her face was dusted with flour, her apron, her hair. She liked to make herself into a fairy-tale woman sometimes—the kindly type with the cottage in the woods who treated all lost souls to the last thing in her larder, forgetting that her own children were clutching at her skirts, crying from hunger.

—You're taking them off the cookie sheets too soon. They're all pulled apart. You've created a house full of gimps, Amanda said.

She was right, of course. All of the cookies, man and beast alike, had legs missing, arms lopped off, or, worse, had undergone complete decapitations. The Christmas trees were missing their peaks, the sleighs their runners, the bells their clappers.

I could see my mother physically recoil from my sister's observation. Very soon she would be on her way up to her room. There she could weep over the invalids she had tried to bring to perfection. The sound of the mail truck pulling up to the house temporarily stopped her. The three of us listened as the mail was pushed through the slot into the drop box.

Before my mother could start to pull her great weight up the back stairs, my sister flew into the foyer, swept up the mail, and appeared in the kitchen again, poised on her toes. She forced the bills into my mother's loose hands. Meanwhile, the last sheet of cookies turned incendiary in the oven, the air foul with bad purpose.

My sister cleared a chair off for her, and Mom sat down to confront the bills.

—Open them, Amanda said.

Since no one else was going to, I retrieved the black, smoky cookies from the oven and dropped them into the sink. My mother found her reading glasses in one of the pockets of her apron and said: I hope the water bill is more reasonable this month.

But when she had the bill out of its envelope, she saw it was even higher.

—There must be a leak, she said, stuffing it into a pocket.

Mom removed her glasses and dabbed a handkerchief around her damp forehead and under her eyes.

—I'll call the City, she said.

—You called the City last month, Mom. And they sent a man out and he checked all the pipes, Amanda reminded her.

—It's that creepy Mr. Graf. He's using all the water, I said.

—Right, pea brain, Amanda said.

—He has the water running all the time. It's like Niagara Falls, for Christ's sake, I said.

—The only thing running is your imagination, Amanda said.

—Maybe he's keeping alligators in the bathtub, I said.

—Probably killer whales, Amanda said, flicking her fingers in my face as if she was sending a bug off into the ether.

—Everything has a way of working out, Mom said, looking around the kitchen, trying to remember what she'd been doing before the world intruded.

—I hope that isn't for school, Amanda said about my failed experiment drowning on the table in a pool of Elmer's glue.

—Wouldn't you like to know? I said. Then I pushed her aside and swept the cards and toothpicks into the overburdened wastebasket. By kinetic force, it slowly spilled onto the floor; no one ever liked to take the garbage out.

—We'll work on it together, Mom said, without asking what my assignment was. But she had no aptitude for science or math, and her mind always wandered if she offered to help with history.

—After I have a little rest. I'll just lie down for a while, she said. It was as if she didn't realize it was evening and that she would be going to bed anyway in another hour or so.

Amanda went over to the oven and opened the door. The sour black smoke coiled toward the ceiling from all the chicken drippings in the broiler.

—I'll talk to Mr. Graf about the water bill, Amanda said. She looked at us as if we'd perish on the spot without another one of her sacrifices.

—Why don't we *all* talk to Mr. Graf? I said, starting toward the door to the maids' quarters—the door my sister had locked the day our tenant moved in.

—I told you he wants to be left alone.

—So what is he, your boyfriend? I sneered.

It was in my mother's nature to sneak off at a moment like that—up a staircase, down a broken garden walk, toward a city bus—anything to avoid the eye of a fight. But she turned to us in absolute delight.

—I'd like to talk with your Mr. Graf; I'd like to meet him.

Her words or maybe just her mood were so incongruous that my sister and I actually stopped. I quickly found a place away from Amanda, and leaned into a pan of cookies on a countertop to watch what was about to happen.

—What? Amanda focused her laser expression on our mother.

—He could probably use the company of someone more his own age, Mom said.

—Not *your* company, Amanda said and turned to go back upstairs.

—But yours? Mom said, stopping her. I saw you go through the back door the other night—and I didn't hear you return for an hour or more.

—He just wanted to show me . . . an old photo album. I guess he was having a sentimental moment or something. You know how people get. I can't believe you're actually spying on me in my own house, Amanda said.

—How old is he? Mom asked.

—I don't know. He has some grey hair. Alright? Amanda said.

—I have some grey hair.

—Look, I have to study, Amanda answered her.

—Certainly you can spare me five minutes, Mom said.

Amanda crossed her arms over her chest and said: What?

—Is he married?

—Is he married?

—And he's happy here? Mom adjusted her sweater in such a way that the bulges of her stomach might vanish altogether.

—He will be if we leave him in peace, Amanda said.

—And you say he was a hypnotist? Mom said.

—Did I say that? Amanda said, considering her fingernails.

—Yessss, you did, I hissed.

—Your father hated hypnotists. He said it was all a fake, my mother said. She smiled at me.

—Was Dad a fake? I asked.

—The worst kind, Mom said.

You could see the way she considered her internal landscape more than us when she answered.

—He couldn't stand his patients. He hated all their complaints, you know. He used to say the world is filled with whiners ready to put money down for the privilege of pissing and moaning into anyone's ear.

—He didn't say that, Amanda said.

—I beg your pardon, Mom said, rearing up.

—Just because he left you doesn't mean he wasn't a good therapist.

—You know, he thought about leaving his practice for years before he actually did.

—All you can think about is that he left *you,* Amanda said.

—No, your grandfather . . . After your father left, your grandfather sent me a number of letters your father wrote to him over the years. Your father had quite a disdain for his profession—not just me, she said, glaring at my sister.

—Did he ever analyze you? I asked.

—Every day of our marriage, Mom smiled in an unpleasant way.

—Really? I asked.

—God, you're so dumb I can't believe it, Amanda said.

—A retired stage performer . . . , my mother said dreamily. I think a certain amount of illusion is a necessary, healthy thing in life. Yes, I think I'll make a point of calling on your Mr. Graf. I've always liked magicians, she said.

It was easy to see the pleasure my mother took in making my sister squirm; most of the time it was the other way around.

—Stop! Both of you just stop it! my sister screamed.

—Stop what? Mom asked her.

—No man's going to save you from yourself! Don't you look in the mirror anymore? You're fat, Mother. F-A-T. OBESE. No man wants to sit around and watch an ugly woman stuff herself on broken cookies!

Amanda grabbed the closest cooling rack. She hurled

the cookies into the air. She threw things down, split things open, tore things apart. My mother ducked into the back stairwell. I headed for the dining room. But Amanda kept going, slamming the oven door repeatedly, shouting and wailing, her words so cruel no one could store them up for later, no one would ever quite remember them.

Before she stopped, she'd broken one of the windows and bent a leg on one of the kitchen chairs. We retreated to our separate rooms, each careful to avoid the others on the way. But that meant no dinner. And when I had to find something to eat, late that night, listening to the creak of the back steps all the way to the bottom, I prayed I wouldn't wake anyone.

There was my mother, asleep on the kitchen floor, a constellation of pans and confusion around her, air blowing hard through the broken window.

I believe she ate each and every one of those pathetic cookies before she nearly died of exhaustion and sugar shock, and then slept a dreamless sleep—because that was the safest kind—waiting for me to come downstairs and cover her with a tablecloth.

My mother had to call in sick the next day at the job she hated. But she was well over her limit of sick days. She held the phone away from her ear as her boss threatened her with unemployment and a poor recommendation to the next job.

I decided to be truant because it was one of those days when it was too surreal, too dishonest to sit in school and play at summing up the world. Instead I rode on elevated trains from one end of town to another on one fare and too many transfers.

But Amanda, she went to school that day. Got an A-plus on her test and stayed out late with her friends, at a pizza party, she said.

That's when I vowed to take Mr. Graf away from my sister.

FIVE

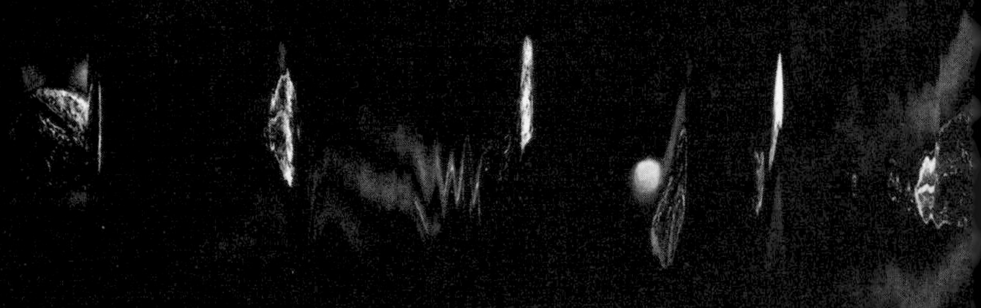

I'M ONE OF THOSE PEOPLE WHO BELIEVE THE Earth will be overtaken by insects someday. Not because I'm a pessimist, and not for personal reasons—like imagining my sister having her day of reckoning with tarantulas—but I think if anyone does, it's the insects who deserve the place. They seldom complain, and if there's mental anguish among them, I can't see it.

That's why I decided I wasn't going to let the man from Chappy's Pest Control into the apartment. I wasn't about to give a leg up to the wrong side. Even though Edith, my sister's secretary, got me on the phone at a vulnerable moment. I was dripping wet from the shower and thinking too much about Mom. Edith said there was a man on his way over and Amanda would cut off my allowance if I didn't let him in.

Edith does that. When she first got hired, her function was to perform secretarial duties, maybe shop for a few Christmas presents, pick up my sister's dry cleaning. Amanda has a way of always getting a little extra from people. But over time, Edith became my sister's henchman. Sometimes I'd tell Edith she was crying wolf with her threats because that was guaranteed to get a rise out of her. And sometimes I pretended I didn't hear the message machine going on, and that nasal voice of hers. But every now and then I cooperated because getting it from her and my sister both was the shits.

I was just going to open the door enough to tell Pest Man to come back another time, so he'd stop leaning on the bell. But when I saw him . . . well, he was pretty young, probably desperate for the job. He wasn't very cute, but he was intense and sexy in a Pest Control kind of way. Someone I could instantly see Sharon going out with. All of her guys were from the fringe; the fringe on the other side of the cloth her mother had spent a lifetime weaving.

Sharon would never buy into the smart-set men her mother had lined up for her. The guys capable of showing off on their polo ponies, ready to take her yachting. She'd grab the waiter instead, the stable boy, the most threatening-looking member of the crew—and fuck him down in his skinny little bunk.

I made Mr. Chappy show his ID through the crack in the door, which was fastened by the chain-lock. He slipped a business card my way with a drawing of a Pied Piper guy with legions of cockroaches trailing after him. I fingered the card and saw that Pest Man's arm was being dragged down by a large black case of death. But the more I saw that impatient pout of his the more I thought of Sharon. I took the chain off the door.

I showed him into the living room and his eyes began to dart around, looking for moving things, poachers, all the deadbeat creatures my sister wanted removed from her life. I asked if he'd like a Coke, though I didn't think we had any. He said he didn't drink Coke—something about it being too toxic—but he could use a glass of water if I had bottled water. I told him to sit down.

I went down the long hall into the kitchen, my wet hair dripping into one of Amanda's shifts. I poured a glass of water from the tap and brought it back to him.

—It's one of those new Italian brands we're trying out. I'd love to have your opinion on it, if you don't mind, I said.

This seemed to warm him to the occasion. He threw one leg over another and sank a little deeper into my sister's easy chair with the gaudy flower print.

—Thanks. So, you're having spider troubles, he said. I watched him open his case and search for his order book.

—Not really.

—Hmmm. I spoke with an Edith Lamont. . . .

—It's my sister; she's the one having the spider troubles.

He smirked and snapped his case shut.

—I'll just take a look around.

—I think she's got wolf spiders, but she says she never sees them. They attack her in bed at night and leave these huge red welts all over her torso, I said.

He headed straight for the bathroom.

—Of course, I suspect something else is going on, I said, trailing after him.

—Such as?

He pushed his flashlight into the private affairs below Amanda's sink. Tampax, bath oils, defunct electric toothbrush.

—It's hard to say, but I think she's allergic to her boyfriend.

—It can happen, he said, backing out and accidentally bumping into me.

After we both mumbled our embarrassment we headed into the dining room.

—Really? You know someone who's allergic like that? I said.

—I think my mother's allergic to my father.

—Does she get the hives?

—Her mouth blisters up whenever they have a fight. She just goes nuts, you know? he said.

—My sister goes nuts. I know.

He asked about my situation, the apartment, my family and all. I told him some of it in a loose, sketchy way, making up things when that was the easiest thing to do. And he probably told me a lie or two. There's a science to dealing with strangers.

As we moved from room to room, I sometimes felt the

warmth of his flashlight inadvertently heat up my skin. It was as if we were working as a team, on safari or something. And then I thought, maybe he wasn't really all that right for Sharon. She'd never agree to go on a blind date and her mother probably saw to any indelicate insect problems in their sprawling apartment years ago. Worse, maybe they'd be allergic to one another and I'd be responsible. I mean, if Sharon fell head over heels in love with him, only to find he was raising massive welts on her body every time she looked at him. . . .

I was so busy trying to work things out for Sharon that it took me a moment to realize we were standing by my sister's bed. The sheets were thrown back, her negligee like a shed skin on the floor, two open condom packages on the nightstand.

My sister was always the careful one, the planner.

I had heard Amanda and Nathaniel come in late, but I'd kept to the study. Avoiding them both all that week, I'd managed to get out of the house each day before my sister woke up. I pretended to go to bed early and hadn't called Nathaniel at the number he gave me. Sharon spent days convincing me that phoning was the worst thing I could ever do. I had to make him sweat for me, die a million deaths, she said. Then I could call. She said seven days. All week I had shifted his card from pocket to pocket when I changed clothes so it rode against my hip constantly. This was the seventh day.

But just the night before I heard them together.

I had actually begun to think he wasn't seeing my sister anymore, after our meeting everyone else had paled out for him, become nonexistent. Especially her. That he had spent his days and nights scouring the metropolis for the girl who fit perfectly into the back seat of a cab.

The wretched thing was, the entire city had started to smell like him. I mean I couldn't ride past my subway stop, drift through a library, or wonder why I was standing in the lobby of a high-rise—confused, confused at best—without suffocating in his cologne, his sex, his unwashed hair, the sour palate of too many martinis.

That's all I could think about until I remembered the man from Chappy's Pest Control.

We were both looking at the empty condom packages next to her bed when I said: My sister has no morals.

I returned to the living room. Joining me near the empty fireplace a couple of minutes later, he said: I'm not really seeing your wolf spiders. But I'll go ahead and do some spraying anyway.

He smiled the smile of complete reassurance; the world would soon be put back into balance.

—The compound I use is one hundred percent environmentally safe. There won't be any need to cover your dishes or food items.

As if I would.

He had some things he needed to get out of his truck and wanted to go out the back door to the alley. I unlocked the bolts and saw him out the door. I was about to give Sharon a call when I realized I hadn't heard the bug man go down the creepy back stairs. My sister was always telling the landlord he better fix those stairs before someone gets hurt and sues the pants off him. She told him he could lose his entire building and it would be like one quick move on a useless board game.

I threw the door open. There was the one hundred percent environmentally safe man, sitting between two great stacks of Amanda's old newspapers. He was just lighting up a joint.

I stood in the doorframe and felt the breeze go through my sister's shift.

—Hi, he said.

He studied my knees through the screen door.

—It gets me into the mood—for killing, he laughed and offered me a hit.

I was going to say no and go back into the apartment and brood about Nathaniel. But I decided to just crouch down next to him for a minute and smell the weed. It's a smell I like, the way some people like gasoline fumes or linseed oil.

We watched the apartments on the other side of the alley. I was always curious to know what those people were doing in their kitchen nooks while Amanda rocked the world on her side. I took a taste, just to pass the time. I kept meaning to ask his name, but then I thought I had and that I'd already forgotten it, so I just waited until he referred to himself by name, but I don't think he ever did.

He talked for a while about recycling. I guess he was

inspired by the papers my sister would probably never haul down the back stairs.

—The Earth is in peril; the environment is a personal mission of mine, he said.

—The bugs you kill don't give a shit about your philosophy. You'll be haunted by angry spirits for the rest of your days.

He chuckled, thinking I was kidding.

I don't know why we ended up making it on my sister's bed of all places. I don't know why I did it with him at all. You know how it is with some people. You just seem to knock in all the wrong places, your nose against their chin, your head against the wall.

He kept talking to me the whole time, like he was trying to make me run faster or jump higher—maybe he wanted to teach me how to hang glide. I mean it was this crazy, low talk—and I couldn't listen to it after a while. And then, when he started to sweat, the whole room was filled with the stench of dying insects.

I wanted to tell him to stop halfway through but I didn't want to get into a fight about it. I needed to see Nathaniel bad.

I felt this guy's whole repugnant body finally repel against mine. When I opened my eyes, he was standing next to the bed. Another one of life's pathetic efforts at reproduction collected in a reservoir, dangling from him like so much DDT. I was so glad it was over.

I stood up and said: You'll have to go. My sister'll be home any minute.

It wasn't true. He could see that much. We could both see that much.

He clutched his abdomen, as if I'd just punched him. As if I'd just used him, cheated on him, turned his head around. Like he mattered that much to want to hurt; like I mattered.

—I'll call you, he said, as he started to dress.

—Sure. Look, I . . . , I said. But all I could do was shrug and go off to the bathroom.

I kept the door ajar until I heard the front door close. It's not that I didn't trust him, but it was my sister's apartment. My only comfort was that I'd kept Sharon from the guy. It would have been a disaster. I know that now. An allergy in the making.

Maybe it was a proximity thing, maybe something of my sister had begun to slowly rub off on me, whether I liked it or not—which I didn't. Maybe it happened because I had to breathe her air all the time again, like I used to before she moved out of Mom's. Except everything had become Amanda's. Amanda's water glasses, Amanda's towels, Amanda's clothes when I forgot to throw mine in the laundry. Anyway, I think I began to develop her intuitive thing, because no sooner had I sent the man from Chappy's down the stairs with its sputtering lightbulbs, than I heard my sister's signal—three rings of the bell—and her animated trudge on the steps. I really didn't know she was coming home just then. She had no regular schedule and typically stayed downtown for events, deadlines, too many conversations. I just felt the urgency to get him out of there because I sensed Amanda was on her way.

I was making her bed in a haphazard fashion, breathing frantic air, when I remembered how disheveled it was when she left the house. The sheets and blankets down around the bottom. I couldn't just throw the covers back to the floor again because she'd see the wet spot. So I managed to bundle all the sheets and the mattress pad up in my arms one second before she stepped through the door.

She hated it if I was in her room, for any reason, even when she was there. Unless she made an express point of inviting me because she suddenly missed me, or missed the idea of family, or felt repentant about something. Apparently I caught her in an expansive mood, light and generous. She even laughed when she saw me, as if the world was an amusing place where nothing should be taken too seriously.

—What's up? she said.

—The bug man came and he suggested we strip the beds because of the spray.

My sister put her briefcase and packages down in the hall and came over to the bed. She sniffed around the bed frame and said: He sprayed in here?

But he hadn't. We'd forgotten about that altogether.

—He got it pretty good, I said.

—I don't smell any insecticide.

She opened a window. What she probably did smell was bug-man sex and had it confused with her own, fetid smells from last night.

—That's because it's one hundred percent environmentally safe.

—Then why do we have to strip the beds, goose? she laughed.

—Well . . . he said we don't *have* to, but that he would, if it was his place. Just as an added precaution. I guess nothing's ever one hundred percent reliable.

—You've got that right, she said.

Always a fatal flaw. We both understood that. I went into her bathroom and dumped the sheets into the hamper for the twice-weekly visit of the surly housekeeper. Everyone who worked for Amanda was surly—with me, at least; rarely with her. When I came back into the room, I realized Amanda was seeing my new hair for the first time. But she had her friendly rifle turned on me, the one with the happy bullets.

She came over and squeezed some of the still-damp ends of my platinum hair in her fingers. Then she stood back and said: I don't think it's bad. In fact, I kind of like it. You shouldn't wear a wig. Just blow-dry it a little.

I screwed up my mouth to thank her and was leaving her room when she sat down on the bare mattress and said: Stay awhile.

—I should get homework started.

—But I came home early to spend time with you, she said. My sister curled a pillow into her lap and leaned into the headboard.

—I've got this paper to write, I said.

Actually, I'd done my homework in a couple of free periods that day.

—I'll help you with it. Come on, I had Edith order Chinese for us while I was en route.

Before I could recoil down the hall, the deliveryman rang the bell. I had to buzz him in and wait while he came up the three flights. Meanwhile, Amanda warmed up her bedroom television with a Thin Man movie. She threw the comforter—the one Mom made when Amanda got married—onto the bed like a picnic blanket. Against my better judgment, I felt myself being pulled into her mood. I ate, knowing it would disappear, the way Chinese food does. And Amanda kept serving me huge platefuls, as if I was incapable of helping myself. When we were knee-deep in goldfish cartons and Nick and Nora's conversation, Amanda asked me to go into the hall and get the packages there. She'd shopped all week on her lunch hours just for me.

I wanted to ask if that meant she hadn't seen Nathaniel all week, since they often had lunch together. But I didn't. She'd picked out six different outfits for me. Not the young sister crap I would have expected, and not the Saks Fifth Avenue stuff Amanda ran through like silk-and-wool water. But things . . . things I realized Nathaniel would like. Maybe he helped pick them out.

On top of this bounty of clothes, she handed me too much money from her sleek black wallet.

—Please get some new shoes and let me know when you need something. I just haven't had enough time to pay attention to you the way I should, she said.

—That's okay, I said.

—I've set up a charge at the little market two blocks

over. All you have to do is call them and have things delivered. But tell them to leave the bags just outside the door. You never really know who these delivery guys are. Were you okay about letting the pest control man in when you were home alone?

There was always the faint hope on weird evenings like that, that my sister had begun to undergo a metamorphosis. I could almost envision a series of slow, torturous surgeries. But it was like wishing the moon would always be at its slender point. Only a suggestion of a moon. That kind of hope just added to my panic.

I jumped up from Amanda's bed, and the carton of sweet-and-sour spilled into the comforter.

—Jesus Christ, I completely forgot about Sharon!! I said.

—Molly! Not the comforter! Fuck!

—I told her I'd meet her at the library at six o'clock. We have this history project.

I ran like hell from Amanda's sacred territory.

—You stay here and help me clean this shit up!!

But I abandoned her. I grabbed my purse. Didn't even think to take something warm to put over her shift—the one she graciously said nothing about my wearing without permission.

I would find out later, many times in fact, that the sweet-and-sour soaked all the way into the mattress. That it drew those spiders to her, hungrier than ever. No matter how she treated the fabric with solvents and tears, no matter how she tried to undo the curse and begged the creatures of the night to haunt my bed instead of hers, they marched on.

I called from the phone booth at the liquor store. The phone rang for a long time. While I waited, I looked at the bottles shaped like Elvis, James Dean, Marilyn, a Cubs baseball bat. Nathaniel finally picked up. All he wanted to know was how long it would take me to get there. It wasn't an afterthought, but he told me to pick up a bottle of whiskey.

I hung up and called a cab. Then I phoned Sharon to square things in case my sister tried to track me. That's when Sharon said we were going to have lunch the next day; she wanted a full report on my bad-girl life.

I didn't know what kind of whiskey to buy and probably spent too much money. The owner's hands moved quickly toward a bottle in a soft purple bag and I saw a cockroach move toward the candy bars. The place was swimming in cockroaches. The owner was used to seeing me in there for ice-cream bars and cigarettes, which, I always told him, were for my sister. He'd never seen me in there with Amanda.

He asked for my ID.

—Sorry. I left it at home. But it's not for me. It's for my sister. Do you want me to get her on the phone?

He looked me over in his sick-drool way and said: That's all right but tell your sister she should come in herself next time.

He slid the bottle into a sack while glancing over at the door, to make sure no one was watching.

—My sister's dying of cancer. The doctor says this stuff

is shit for her, but I'm not going to be the one to tell her "No," you know?

He had this look, like he was suddenly bubbling and churning with commiseration. I was sure he was about to tell me some horrible personal tragedy, when I heard the cab outside. I gave him a huge smile and said: You're very kind. Most people aren't. I'll let her know how kind you are.

If there's one thing I'm good at, it's memory games. My father made a point of teaching me how to use word associations, tiresome rhymes, little mathematical tricks when I was very small. This would give me, he believed, the advantage of passing tests and beating the system—whatever the system happened to be at the time. He loathed anything of a collective nature, anything that smacked of human order: schools, unions, churches, even hospitals. As much as he loved books, he hated libraries—Dewey decimal and all that.

Anyway, he used to do this thing with me, where he'd set up a tray of objects in his study and take me there blindfolded. Once he removed the blindfold, I'd have a second or two to study the tray. Then he'd take me out of the room again. I was supposed to give him a complete list of everything I'd seen. He'd do it over and over. Each time with new objects, new arrangements. Adding to the number, multiplying the tricks. Eventually I got to the point, after many confessions of stupidity on my part and strange threats on my father's part, where I wouldn't miss a single item on the tray. It was how he made me practice—the way other kids learned an instrument or dance steps or sending a clean pitch over home plate.

It left me with a feeling about blindfolds. That they aren't about games of spin-the-bottle, or long car rides to hideouts, or executions before a firing squad. Blindfolds are old, silk ties of dark fabric that can be wound around the head more than once. They smell of pipe tobacco and urgency. They're the meaning of the word "memory" and they're a thing of torture and shallow breath.

I found myself wondering, that night, if Nathaniel knew about my aversion, if my sister told him something. Or if he, too, had developed this kind of intuitive sense from spending too much time with Amanda.

When I saw Nathaniel waiting outside his building, I put on my sunglasses—my only disguise other than my hair. I'd dropped one of the contact lenses in the cab when I tried to put them in, and I knew I'd never find it or want to put it back in my eye if I did. I'd forgotten to grab makeup of any substance before I left, so I feared he'd recognize me immediately.

But I kept telling myself he'd only seen the real me a couple of times at Amanda's. On my way out or slipping into the kitchen. Except that one time when he offered to take me on his motorcycle, but the hall was dark, only a tiny spot of light from the ceiling. And he was standing behind me, talking close to my head.

He paid the driver and took my hand. I stumbled a couple of times, getting in the elevator and again in the hall because of the dark glasses. Maybe he thought I'd been drinking, but maybe he'd been drinking so much himself he didn't notice. In either case he was patient with me.

He'd left his apartment door cracked open and now he stepped aside to let me enter. The only light in the room was from the hood over the stove. The kitchen and living room formed one large space. Where my sister's apartment choked on floral patterns and large, stuffed pillows and childish, uncertain art, Nathaniel's was modern to the point of steel. Charcoal leather couches, icy glass tables, a wall of sound equipment to blow the dust off the clouds, a couple of abstract, black-and-white photos. A boxing match was on the television without the sound. He offered me a drink.

The fumes from the whiskey he put in my hands touched my face in a confusing way.

—I've got an appointment in a while, he said.

I thought of telling him that ever since that day in the taxi, he'd become this painful series of impulses shooting through my body day and night. But I didn't even say I'd missed him. I knew, if Sharon knew anything, that that's how you lose a guy.

—Yeah, I have an appointment in a while myself, I said.

He winked at me. I didn't understand what his wink meant. That's the advantage Nathaniel had with people, keeping them curious, drawing them in a little further in order to find out. Like those men who know how to pull you into a sideshow, get you to watch things you feel uncertain about, maybe a little ashamed.

He said: I thought you'd call sooner.

—I couldn't get away. Someone's . . . dying, I said, spinning the lone ice cube in my drink.

—I'm sorry. Close to you?

—Yes, but I'd rather not talk about it, I said.

I still believe there's a value to mystery. Unexplained disappearances, secrets held back, sudden unexpected reunions. . . . He smiled as if he might know my mystery was made for the occasion, then he looked over at the men beating each other in silence on the television set.

—It's my sister, I said, to convince him.

—That's terrible, he said, still watching the fight. But I could see the way my words affected him.

—Cancer, I said.

—Cancer, he said, shaking his head, as if everyone he'd ever loved had had cancer.

That's when I thought he didn't know my sister was Amanda—but then maybe he thought we had another sister or that I was referring to a sister in another way.

He got up and offered to top off my drink but I hadn't touched it. I wasn't much of a drinker. I liked the smell more than anything. Not Nathaniel. He drank plenty, and I doubt he ever took time to smell the stuff.

—Hurt your eyes? he said.

—My eyes?

—Sunglasses, he said, tapping on the rims.

—No . . . I had an eye exam today. Light hurts them.

—Even the light from the television? he asked.

—Yes, I said.

I asked about his job. I really didn't understand what

he did except that it was in construction, high-rises and stuff. Was it estimates? Negotiations? Maybe contracts. I wasn't sure, but Sharon told me all the big construction in the city had something to do with the mob.

Just as I was treating the death in my family, Nathaniel preferred not to talk about his work. It had been a long day, he said. Too long.

He leaned over and slipped a hand up my sister's shift. I wanted to make love with that man up one side of his apartment and down the other, but worse than that, I needed to talk. I couldn't say about what. I just needed to talk with Nathaniel.

I pulled his hand away and kissed it and said: What would you think about a man who slept with his brother's wife?

—What would I think? he said.

—I mean, what if it was your brother and his wife?

—And I slept with her? he said, easing into the couch a little, reaching for his glass on the coffee table.

—Exactly, I said.

—And you want to know . . . ? he said, his eyes focused on the fight again.

—Do you consider it . . . a sin?

This made him laugh and he said: I'm afraid I don't see the world in terms of sin and repentance.

I thought this over. The larger boxer had begun to hammer into the smaller one's face. Nathaniel said "Oomph," as if his own face had been smashed.

—Alright, then . . . morally wrong? I said.

—Are you sleeping with your dying sister's husband?

—No, I. . . . There isn't anyone else, I said, and hated myself the minute I said it. I mean, it's not that I wanted him to think there was anyone else, because that's the way you cheapen yourself with a guy. At the same time, I didn't want him to get the idea that the world revolved around him—because that would scare him off if anything would.

While I scraped along the edge, I realized my answer meant little to him. He was more concerned with returning to my question.

—Is this a party game, then?

—You don't know, do you? I smiled.

—Don't know what? he said, looking at me again. He leaned over and kissed my ear.

—How you'd feel about it, I insisted, trying to ignore his mouth.

—How can I? Did my brother just run off with my life's savings after burning my house down and raping my three daughters? Did he separate from his wife and I fell in love with her and we just don't know how to tell him yet? Was I dead drunk? Too sober? Did my brother just die and I'm trying to console his widow? You haven't given me enough to work with.

—So then you think, under certain circumstances, it might be considered . . . permissible? I said.

—Permissible? I'm no closer to permission than I am to sin. But would it make sense, could it happen, even if I felt bad the next day? Probably.

He stared at me for a long time. I was aware of the reflection against my sunglasses, of two men weakening each other, bleeding against each other. I would try every possible avenue into him that night, questions, more questions. I thought I was trying to find out who he was, what made him tick, as if there was one question that would suddenly reveal everything. But looking back, I know it was all about Amanda. I had to find out if she possessed him and if she did, to what degree.

—Do you have a brother? I asked.

—Nope.

—A sister?

—Not a one, he said.

—So maybe you can't understand what that kind of relationship . . . , I began.

But I could see by the look he made out of the corner of his eye that he was done with that line of questioning.

—Are your folks alive? I said.

—Last time I checked, my dear inquisitor, he said, sliding his hand up my skirt again.

And though I was dying for him, my body racing, everything inside nuclear with aching, I was still trying to pull back, because I wanted to talk with Nathaniel.

I know I had this fantasy that we'd stay up so late we'd suffocate on words till we didn't know who was speaking anymore. Then we'd have to make love or threaten suicide. It's hard to explain. Like looking in the mirror so long your eyes become something else, you become something else. I wanted to become something else inside Nathaniel's eyes.

But everything we said that night was so tight and choppy, as if it were resisting, moving away from us, from me. I drank and looked at him. But maybe he didn't see my look. Maybe he didn't see that I was thinking of running off. Because suddenly he was standing above me.

—Alright, my turn, he said.

I watched him go into the other room. He came back, holding something behind him. His body leaned a little. I think he was getting pretty drunk.

—Close your eyes, he said, and sat next to me again.

—Are they closed? he asked, staring into my sunglasses.

I said yes, but they weren't; I figured he couldn't tell. But he reached out and pulled my glasses off before I could stop him.

—You have two different-colored eyes. You know, they burned women at the stake for less during the Salem witch trials.

—It's a hereditary thing, I said.

He must have known me as Molly then, when he saw my eyes. He had to. But if he did, I guess it was like Sharon said about masquerading, playing along but knowing.

—My sister and my mother have the same thing, I said.

—Now keep them shut, he said.

I felt the cloth against my face. His fingers made a quick knot at the back of my head, pulling my hair. A sailing panic went through my body and I wanted to rip the blindfold from my face. I had love and sacrifice jumbled up together, like sin and forgiveness. I hadn't learned to see things as cleanly as he had. I kept thinking that my sister had sold herself or sold me in the bargain, sold off our terror for a run with temporary love.

—Is this what you want? I said.

—This is what you want, he said.

Unlike my father's blindfold, Nathaniel's was thin, almost light, and let the shadows of soundless boxers move across my vision.

I began to think that that's what it was all about—that he wanted to make love with me while these men pummeled and crushed each other, bled their hopes and winnings away, until someone was knocked into a senseless state. Nathaniel would be able to see what he was doing and I was to pretend I didn't.

He moved away from me. I could tell by the sound of his ice knocking the sides of his glass. I heard a curtain being reeled in or out and a click, the sound of his sliding glass door to the balcony. As it moved along its track I was reminded that Nathaniel lived four stories up.

—Can you see the lake? I called.

—Not yet, he whispered as he came close again. Then farther away. He turned off the light above his stove.

—I'm afraid of heights, I said.

—All the more reason to keep your eyes shut, he said. He slipped a hand into one of mine. Then he made me turn around and I felt one of my shins knock into the coffee table. I didn't say anything; I'm not sure why. He guided me across his carpet and I heard the sounds of the lake almost smothered by the rush of traffic along the Drive. A wind came up hard as we got onto his balcony, my balance awkward. I felt my nipples stiffen inside my sister's dress, something crazy inside my sister's boyfriend's head.

I really thought his balcony would just end without a

railing, which he would forget to tell me was under construction in his brilliant, drunken state. He'd just let me drift out to the edge with my confessions and impulses. I was relieved to bump into another table with the same knee—to be grounded by a pain that seared into the first bruise. He closed the door behind us.

I was wrong about the railing. Because he took my hands and placed them against the cold metal. I held on like one of those punch-drunk airplane riders, holding onto the nose of a plane in a goddamn air show.

—Don't let me die, Nathaniel, I said.

—Shhh, he said.

He began to reposition my feet, spreading my stance out. The air rushed up my legs, the wind slapped Amanda's dress against my body.

—Why the hell do you want to live so badly? he said. He moved his hands up my inner thighs.

—I don't know, I said. I began to think about mass murderers—honest to god, that's what came to me. How we all go into shock when they mow through a fast-food restaurant with their old Vietnam weapons, cutting a swath through the people at the counters, through the plastic playground equipment attached to the restaurant, driving people into freezers, fleeing into parking lots. But no one cares about the single, solitary death anymore. The girl released into her own mind from a four-story balcony before she's painted along the Drive by cars and limousines, or scared into the next life by bad water and bloated, cancerous fish in an ailing lake.

—I need to know, he said, suddenly on me with his

mouth. Talking against me with his mouth, trying to get me to talk with his tongue high up on me. The cold air and his tongue pushing inside.

—Because . . . because I don't want to be with the dead, I said.

Before I understood any of it, he became painfully gentle. He picked me up, and maybe I was ready to be thrown from any height then, because I wasn't afraid at that point. He lowered me onto a lounge chair, and made love to me in a way that pulled the consciousness out of me.

When it was all over, he took off my blindfold and held my face in both his hands. He was propped on his elbows, hovering above me.

Neither of us could talk.

When I slowly began to recognize the weight of his body next to mine, I understood we were both tired, more tired than either of us would say. I pulled myself away to let him sleep, and went into his apartment to look for a blanket. I found a large down comforter in his bedroom and dragged that out to him. I was standing in the doorway, about to move outside to cover him, to cover us, wondering if it was safe to sleep the night through on the balcony. I worried that he might walk in his sleep, that I might, when the phone rang.

I was going to smother it with anything I could find, my body if I had to, but Nathaniel stirred.

—Jesus, he said.

He leapt up to get the phone, kissing me so I'd move aside from where I blocked the doorway.

It was Amanda. He called her Mandy. I thought she always hated that name. She was his appointment. The way he looked at me as he talked to her, I was terrified that he would put things together and tell her. What he didn't know, couldn't know, was that if he just waited, if we both waited Amanda out, she'd tire of him before long. Then she wouldn't even care. She'd throw him to me like an article of clothing she had no use for anymore.

But all he said was a couple of distracted "Sorry"s. They made some rough plans for another meeting and he was off the phone.

He gave me this look, like he was about to ask me to leave. I didn't say a thing, but watched him take the comforter from my hands and carry it back to the bedroom.

I looked around the balcony for my clothes but couldn't find Amanda's shift. I think the wind took it. There was no other explanation. It was all for the best. It could never be her dress anymore—I couldn't watch her move inside it. And it wasn't mine. It was his more than anyone's. Or the city's—a flag to the impossible spring. I looked over the dark lake, made mysterious by the flood of lights burning all over his apartment building. After a while I went back inside.

Nathaniel would find something for me to wear home; I wasn't worried about that. I gathered the rest of my things and stood near the front door, waiting to see if he would come back or if he'd fallen asleep.

That's when I realized he was saying my name—well, the name Yvonne, anyway. I don't know how many times he said it. I crept down the hallway, as if I was somewhere I didn't belong. There he was, calling me into his shower—

a large, glass-enclosed shower big enough for a family. The water streamed over his head, his eyes closed, and I dropped everything I held on the floor and joined him.

I can't say if it was a trick of the mind, but I've often thought he was crying that night. Holding onto me in the mad rush of water and crying.

Then he soaped my body like I was a child. He turned me around and let the water rinse me off. He wrapped me in a huge towel and carried me into the bed he'd made again, the comforter pulled back at one corner to let us slip inside.

Before we fell asleep, his arm tight around me, he said: I'll find out where you come from.

SIX

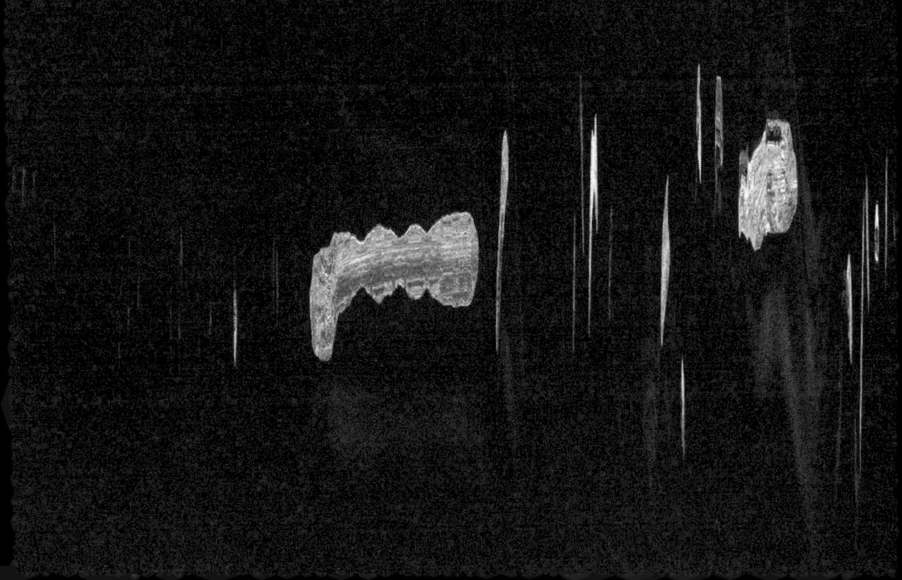

THERE WAS A POINT WHEN MY MOTHER STOPPED CARING for her appearance the way a gone-mad person would suddenly stop feeding a pet they'd nurtured into complete dependence. She was in her late forties then. I think it was her forty-eighth birthday, when only a single card came from a cousin she hadn't seen in years. Nothing arrived UPS. My sister forgot altogether, staying over late at a friend's house. I got her a vegetable chopper that looked as if it could do anything in the world, but couldn't grip a single carrot.

My mother turned to me with her cousin's card still in its envelope.

—Birthdays just dry up like the flesh, I guess, she said.

She threw the unopened card on top of the overflowing trash in the kitchen and headed up to her bedroom. The dull vegetable blades were scattered across a countertop. I don't think she bothered with makeup for a long time after that. The long battle to fit into the nicer dresses and suits in her closet—her married clothes, she called them—seemed to be over.

That's why it was so odd, one day, to see her poised on the back steps of the manor in a pair of black patent leather heels. It's funny, but I try to see the dress she wore, the stockings, any other detail of her outfit, a piece of jewelry. Yet all I can see are those black-mirror shoes standing out in the last push of twilight. Her feet were crossed at the ankles, something seductive, something terribly wrong about the height of her heels.

She didn't see me crouched down in the yard. I was hiding behind the pile of rusting lawn furniture Amanda made a boy haul home from the Salvation Army; something she would never find time or energy to refurbish. It was in the nature of the manor to gather rags and remnants into its skirts, certainly to resist all refinements. If cans of paint were purchased, they were opened to check for a color match and then left to cake over and dry without use. The turpentine cans were always empty, the shears blunt, the hammer separated from its handle and nails could never be found, though it seemed like someone was always buying nails.

During the summers the sunset had a way of coming in low through the trees and suddenly lighting up all the windows in the back of Wharton Manor. It was like a movie set, painted red, with light almost to the chimneys. I knew what my mother was up to. The light moving down her face, trying to paint over the rough edges of her age. The way she leaned into the porch railing, like a woman embarking on her first cruise to a foreign land. At a loss for words, for expression, self-conscious. Not really hopeful about meeting anyone, unable to stay in her own country anymore. Maybe she was thinking about the way people just disappear midvoyage, jealously recalling the story of a friend who met and married the captain of her first cruise so that she never did have to brave foreign soils, foreign tastes or tongues, in order to find love.

My mother was lit up for a dance with death on her own back steps. She knocked so loudly on Mr. Graf's door, I saw her try to shake the pain in her hand away. She waited awhile, moving her shoes about on the top step.

It was merciful that the light began to change, to shelter us both. She tried again. The door began to open. I could almost feel it give way as if my hand was pushing against the wood. There was an exchange. I saw her turn to balance her way down the steps in those shoes. Then he must have said something, because she stopped and looked up at him for a long time. I still couldn't make out his face in the dark entry, the door never open more than a crack. She went back up the steps and in the door, looking around before she shut it, watching too hard for Amanda.

I came around the side of the house, moving low. It was

impossible to see into any of Mr. Graf's windows—I'd tried that more than once. The dark curtains were pulled taut to the edges. I felt espionage in my blood like hot-pepper flakes as I returned to the front of the house, and I wondered if I could ever keep such a divine secret from Amanda. My mother had left a note on the fridge—Amanda was at her after-school job at the newspaper and planned to spend the night with a friend. Mom claimed to have some function to attend that could keep her out pretty late. There was advice for me on keeping lights burning, doors locked, playing the television and radios LOUD so anyone approaching the house would think several people were at home and all too busy to be burgled.

I had thought about drilling a hole from my side of the house to his to create a peephole, but I was still looking for the old drill bits that went with the drill. And then most of the time I wasn't sure if Mr. Graf was in or out or sleeping or restless—if he was conducting experiments.

All week I had been thinking about the set of skeleton keys I'd found in the pantry. One afternoon, when I couldn't stand it any longer, I began to test them in the lock that separated the two parts of the house. After a nervous process of elimination, one of them worked as quiet as the moon turning in the sky.

I opened the door between us and took off my shoes and socks. I entered Mr. Graf's private passageway.

All that time, I had expected to find rat-sized balls of dust moving through the drafty hallways, spiders big as eyeballs suspended from every doorway, the reek of his experiments. Maybe even a zombie-like character hypnotized into service. Most of all I expected equipment—strange-looking, scientific apparatus. Not just vials and Bunsen burners and things to dredge and pump the bathtub, but dreadful machines to draw any weak creature into the darker side of her personality: moving bull's-eyes and mesmerizing spirals painted onto flat plates spinning in an effort to draw out the disturbed tune of a luckless soul. Instead, I found the halls swept and still, recently mopped, the dark wainscoting oiled to a mirror-like presence.

I did not have much experience with men my father's age and older. My father had never been a social man by nature and though he attended the occasional lecture and even joined an athletic club for a time, he never invited people to the house. (Neither did my mother, probably to fall in line with his way of thinking.) My grandfathers on both sides had died at relatively young ages and the only uncles I had lived far away—or stayed far away.

Once a year or so it was my father's habit to spend a month of intense labor on my "development," beginning with simple mind-games and ending in complex puzzles. He talked to me in low tones, taught me things I could never store whole. They all seemed so wise, so important. Inevitably, just as I began to realize our closeness and think we might spend the rest of our days in pursuit of good memory together, he'd abruptly recede into his own work. He would then treat me as if I was a distant relative's child paying a short visit—someone best left to my mother's mind.

But as unfamiliar as I was with the habits and smells and natures of older men, I couldn't believe how tidy the renter's rooms were, how airy everything felt. All the rooms were open, except the one at the far end, where, I was sure, he sat with my mother: the giveaway light under the door, the faint sound of talk.

I began my search with a small flashlight. I had plenty of experience by then, of moving over a wooden floor in an almost soundless way. I told myself I really didn't care if they caught me. It was surprising to realize that the open doors lead to empty rooms. Even the closets were bare. The bathroom door, which was cracked open, had a worn-clean tub and a towel hung straight to dry.

As I got close to the shut door, I wondered if that room was just as bare as the others. I tried to imagine my mother and Mr. Graf sitting on the floor. She would spend her entire visit worried about how she was going to get up in a graceful way. Had he trapped her in one of his experiments and she thought no one would hear her if she called out?

I was fretting over what to do when I heard a noise, like a single book falling to the floor. Then another, I thought. There isn't any other sound I hate more, and I stopped listening for their conversation and began to think of my father.

The memories I had of him were like pieces from a set of badly chipped china. Something grudgingly handed down from my sister and mother. The set, when laid out, was oddly incomplete. But I felt an attachment to certain pieces, dishes designed for dream meals, not really capable of sustaining me. The shape of a gravy boat, the feel of its long lip curling into a spout, something I could recognize with my eyes shut, without anyone's prompting.

The one memory that was impassable was of my father inspecting his books. Hundreds, maybe thousands of volumes and tomes and series and imprints. Stacked into towers, bridges, tables, pedestals, walkways, statues, chairs, and sofas around our house. Since my father, I was told, did not like to visit the public library and shunned the hospital associations that could have provided handsome medical libraries, and since he disappeared from career and home life before the Information Age could stuff him with unending knowledge, he felt he must purchase every single book he had the slightest fascination with, the mildest curiosity about. Most of them came by post, in plain wrappers. Many were never opened but stacked high, waiting. There was a smirk of satisfaction as he touched their spines, and, I imagine, considered their ability to consume every portion of our living space.

I began to hurry back toward my side of the house. But before I got there, I heard the door swing open. My mother backed into the hall, soaked in harsh light, her ankles turning in from the pressure of her high heels. She was pulling her outfit away from her body at the rear, as if she was trying to pull herself from the room. She began to close the door, all the while smiling idiotically, at Mr. Graf, I presumed—he never stepped into the hall with her. As she turned to go, she saw me standing there.

She started to call my name but stopped and closed the door the rest of the way, her expression wiped clean. I turned my flashlight on her. She made frantic hand movements, as if to shoo me back to the safe side of the house.

I went back out the door I'd come through and locked it as before. My stomach in a flurry, I returned the keys to their hiding place. She went out the back door and all the way around to the front of the house.

When my mother walked into the living room it was as if she'd just gotten home from a day of work. She kicked her shoes off and went into the kitchen. I followed and watched her soak a cool rag to place at the back of her neck while the teakettle heated.

I spread out my homework on the kitchen table across from her, not expecting much of a dinner, planning to rummage in the fridge.

Neither of us said a word the entire evening until one of us stubbornly said: Goodnight.

A week went by before I could catch Amanda at the right moment to talk. I still wasn't sure if I was going to tell her about Mom's meeting with Mr. Graf. Sometimes I think Amanda must have figured it out, Mom was acting so weird—one minute sobbing on her bed without even closing her door, then suddenly jumping up and beginning a harried search for a pair of stockings without a run. I could hear her lament over the way the perfume on her dressing table was going to alcohol. And there were the nights I'd find her dancing in the ballroom, when she thought the house was quiet. Something she hadn't done since we'd first moved into the manor.

Amanda was in the bathtub, about to shave her legs,

and I discovered, *almost* by accident that she had forgotten to lock her bathroom door.

—Excuse me! she said.

—That's all right, I'm just looking for a bar of soap, I said.

—I got the last one.

I crouched by the cabinet under the sink, rummaging, dawdling, trying to gather my thoughts down by the drain catch.

—I don't keep soap under the sink, she said.

—I know. I thought there might be a little remnant. Any old sliver will do.

—Peculiar child, she said.

She pulled one of her legs out of the bubble bath and balanced it on the rim of the tub. I watched her soap that chunky thing with an ample bar of soap, to get it ready for the razor.

—I have to talk with you, Amanda.

—Jesus Christ, are you still here? she said, to vex me; I was in plain sight.

—I have to talk with you about Dad.

—Fuck! You made me cut myself.

—It's probably the razor. I . . . saw Mom using it the other night, I said.

It wasn't true but Amanda gave the razor a terrified look.

—That's disgusting. How could she do that? This is my personal razor. Not hers. Not yours. Would you get the razor blades out of the cabinet? Look at the way she gummed this up. I could throw up. And an old hand towel off the bottom shelf and a bandage. Not the big ones. The little ouchless circles.

—I love the ouchless circles, I said and proceeded to gather all the necessary supplies while she tried to quiet herself. She sank deeper into the tub and watched the thin stream of blood taint her bubbles.

Whenever I proved to be helpful to her it seemed to crack open a small door close to her heart. I poured her a cold cup of water and, at her request, placed it on the ledge by the tub. As soon as she was settled again with more hot water added to the bath and the razor poised with a new blade, she said: What's this about Dad?

—He has to be dead, I said.

She smiled at me and said: I don't think so, Molly.

—Because . . . ?

—Because of my dreams.

—But he has to be dead or he'd get in touch, I said.

—Not necessarily.

—Why not necessarily? I said.

—Sometimes . . . men just disappear. I've had dreams of him and he looks healthy, rested, happier than he's ever been. Really, she assured me, drawing the razor down one leg.

—Well, I had a dream he shot himself in the head and all these tiny little books came tumbling out of his skull, wrapped in plain brown paper, never opened. Millions of books, I said.

Amanda laughed.

—I can understand why you'd have such a dream, she said, trying to look sympathetic.

I wondered if my breasts would get as big as my sister's and float like awkward ships in my bath water; I hoped not.

—Remember at the house before Wharton Manor? Remember when you and I took the train to stay with Mom's friend Sheryl?

That was just after Dad left.

—What about it? she said.

—There was new grass in the backyard when we came back from that trip, I said.

—Yeah, that's when I understood why Dad just couldn't put up with her anymore, why he had to leave. A perfect lawn. I mean, perfect, and she ripped it up and put in the world's most expensive sod. Just to turn around and sell the house. I'm still pissed about it.

—I didn't think there was anything wrong with the old grass either. Amanda?

—What? she scowled.

—Do you think there's something buried under that lawn, at that old house?

She gave me a look, as if I'd finally said something intelligent.

—I wouldn't be surprised.

—I . . . felt lumps, I said.

—Come on, she said, trying to unwind, sinking a little into her water and studying me through the slits of her eyes.

There are some things you wouldn't want to make up.

—Really. Lumps.

—If I remember correctly, we weren't even supposed to walk on the new sod.

—But I did and I got so scared I wouldn't go out in the yard at all until the house sold. And you know what?

—What, pest? she said, turning the hot water on with her toes and finally closing her eyes in the luxury of her private tub, hoping to shut out my revelations.

—I think Dad's buried under that grass.

She sat up suddenly, sputtering: You think she killed our father?

Water slipped over the edge of the tub onto the floor.

—No, I just . . . I don't know. Maybe she didn't want to tell us he died. He probably had a heart attack or something.

—You're so dumb. Throw a towel down to soak up the water, Moll.

—Let's go back to the old house and dig up the lawn and see.

There were things I said to goad Amanda. But she understood that look I got when I was telling her a dreadful truth. I wondered if she had any idea how relieved I was to finally tell someone.

—We can't do that, Molly. People live there. The house belongs to someone else. There are probably always lumps when a new lawn goes in.

—But I'm sure Dad is out there somewhere.

—You're working yourself up over nothing, Molly.

—Alright, Miss High-and-Mighty, if you're so sure you know everything, if Dad ran off to get away from Mom, why doesn't he get in touch with *us?* Tell me that, huh?

I was still unwilling to throw a towel down to soak up the water.

—I'm not sure if I can answer that, she said.

—Of course you can't! Because he's dead and buried in our old backyard. Because even if he hated Mom's guts, he wouldn't hate *us!*

I didn't wait for her to call me back in a gentle way; she wasn't going to do that. As I ran down the stairs I could hear her bleat my name and thrash around in the tub. I hoped she'd have a heart attack right there and drown in her own leg-blood.

I ran out to the garden and found a shovel. I guess a psychologist would say that what I did next was a ritualized act, a pathetic form of compensation. The hole I dug that night wasn't at the old house but at the manor. Right next to the cat grave where Amanda's prissy Siamese was buried.

Too quickly I met the resistance of poor soil. Wharton Manor was tough down to the bone; it suffered from too many years of neglect. When I could no longer penetrate the ground, I decided my father wasn't a very tall man. And after I gave it another serious effort, that he wasn't a very wide man or a very deep man.

When I finished, I took the only picture I could find of him and put it in the mock grave. I found some candles and stuck them in the ground. The cross I made out of old fencing, nailed together with thumbtacks; I couldn't find any nails. "The Lord Is My Shepherd" was the only prayer I could think of. I didn't know all of the words, but the intention was the important thing.

Amanda watched me from the bathroom window. Mom saw me from the kitchen. I thought of Mr. Graf and wondered if he was looking at me as well. At the same time, the house appeared vacant, really—the way that house could be. As if everyone had found a shallow grave for the night.

A few days later, when I saw my mother lying in bed as she did after work—stockings off, a washcloth over her eyes—I got in bed with her. I curled into one of her thin pillows and let my body be pulled in toward hers. There was something about her weight and the age of the mattress, almost a magnetic force. The radio was on so soft you couldn't really tell what the voices were saying. The sky was that early-evening blue that makes you sorry. I thought about how we were more like impressions than real people in that kind of light.

I said: I had a funeral for Dad in the backyard the other day.

I wanted her to tell me something, if there was something to tell, about my father. About the backyard of the old house.

But all she said was: Mmm.

It was sort of a sound, maybe just her breathing.

—I buried his picture, I said, still waiting.

She moved her hand to find mine and held it for a while.

—It's better that way, she said.

—To forget him? I said.

—Yes. It's better to forget him.

—You don't think he'll ever come back, do you, I said, more as statement than question.

—No, I don't. It's best to forget him, like you're doing. But then you've always been the sensible one, the charitable one.

—Did he hate you?

My mother's thumb ran back and forth over my knuckles and I breathed in the scent of her hair, without knowing what flower it was.

—He hated the part of himself that was me, after a while, she finally said.

Then she added: But that isn't why he left.

—Why did he leave? I asked.

—I'll tell you someday, she said, letting my hand go and drawing hers in under her body.

I wanted to ask her if she had hated my father so much she wanted to kill him. And in the same breath I wanted to ask her if she was falling in love with Mr. Graf; if she'd want to kill him someday, too.

But she needed to rest or she'd never recover from another day. And then she'd start the next day barely able to swallow or breathe or sit on the toilet, after a night of battling that fatigue. And then she'd lose another job, miss another occasion, fall further off the Earth.

I also knew she wouldn't give me much of an answer. She made me feel so terribly sorry, I had to back off. I had to accept her somedays as if that was it. Because she had this way of pushing questions off her as if they were strange insects or a quick drizzle that wanted to cling about her shoulders.

SEVEN

SHARON FOUND ME LOITERING OUTSIDE FRENCH CLASS, trying to work on the symptoms of a good illness. Anything to avoid Madame's pug-ugly face, third period. I had a thin bar of soap tucked under one arm in case they used a thermometer on me down in the office. Soap was supposed to make the mercury jump—the French conjugations fly.

She leaned into the bank of grey lockers and sneered at the cheerleaders heading toward the locker room.

—Both our names are on the "list" today. We might as well skip and go for coffee.

I didn't ask her which list; I was always on one or another.

I lifted my arm and we both watched the soap fall out of my dress and land near my feet. Sharon appreciated tricks like that.

—I saw it on a late-night movie, I said, explaining its purpose.

There was a guy sitting hall duty by the exit where we planned to escape. He was a senior named Raymond Hollister. Sharon told me he'd been holding his dick in his hand for her since kindergarten.

Hollister was the kind of guy who didn't have a damaged bone in his face; he had a demeanor that suggested there was nothing beyond repair. There was something absolutely pristine about him. Not stupid or frivolous, just left to his own resources, like Sharon.

As we approached, he looked up from his book. I watched him massage one of his thighs with the flat of his hand, and smile as if he didn't want to but couldn't help himself.

—You never saw us, Sharon said to him.

I expected him to have a quick comeback, something disingenuous to fill the space. But Hollister's quiet attention was on me. He gave me this look, as if there was something he couldn't quite find the words to tell me. Sharon nudged me so I'd go out the door first.

When we were outside, she put her arm around my shoulders and I looked back through the large plate-glass windows at Hollister who continued to follow our movements.

—Hollister has the hots for you, Sharon said.

We both laughed and I waved to him before Sharon and I trekked over the football field. There was something about hearing you were the object of a guy's peak sexual drive. Even if you'd never given the guy a single thought. Sharon went on about it until I felt like a bolt of lightning across that poor boy's sky. All I did was push hard on the emergency door and suddenly I was dancing in the body of a stranger.

—His parents own Hollister's, Sharon said.

Hollister was a big name in the city, if you were tracking big names. That was something Sharon's mother did in an effortless way. She, in turn, tried her best to instill the values of a healthy class system in her daughter. I think it cramped Sharon's brain with the trivia of an incestuous society.

—They're both alcoholics; both total pains in the butt. It'll happen to Ray in time. He'll become a drunken business mogul with a temper like a lapdog, years of hair-transplant surgery stretching out ahead of him.

—So I shouldn't trouble myself? I said.

Sharon described his future wife, the young deb who'd be handpicked by Mr. and Mrs. Hollister.

—She'll be an anorexic thing, unable to function unless she's in the middle of purchasing some useless article for one of her houses. Under heavy sedation, she'll bear three children, who'll be raised by a Norwegian nanny in a far region of one of their mansions. And she'll spend her afternoons whining through her adenoids to bored women named Buffy, Muffy, and Cottontail.

I held my sister's jacket open with both hands. There

was the hope that the cold spring air would clear my soul of the rabbit set and the school they'd built for their inbred children. We walked over to the bakery where we had a way of drinking too much strong coffee.

Sharon wanted a table next to the photomural of the Swiss Alps. The only windows were small and high, the city outside muffled, invisible.

—So?

—What? I said.

—Come on, Molly. Your date. The older man.

Sharon knew she'd be dead by the time she was twenty, like me; she was the closest I could come to a friend in that school. But I knew about secrets. How they seep from friend to friend like an intimate virus until half the school is wheezing with the news, itching to tell. I also knew I owed Sharon for the hair and the makeup. The torn lavender jacket lay in a heap on my bedroom floor, smelling of Nathaniel, the pants stinking of lake water.

If I didn't tell, she'd be pissed. Then I'd suddenly become the girl who gets ganged up on in the locker room, shunned in the lunchroom. I'd be the poor kid on a wasted scholarship. The one with an obese mother who had to be sent away to die; the father who walked out on his family. I would, in short time, have the social prospects of an earthworm on a hot sidewalk. But if I stayed in Sharon's favor, I would remain a slightly exotic thing.

Sipping at the hot espresso, I leapt from one of those high buildings of the mind.

—I'm paralyzed with love, I said rather grimly.

Sharon had switched from American cigarettes to thin,

European cigars that smelled of old parking lots and lost tires. She blew one of her "Go on"s into the air and cracked her knuckles against the edge of the table.

—That's all there is to tell, I said. My hands trembled as I reached for a packet of sugar.

—I've always wanted to be paralyzed with love, Sharon said. She pulled one of the extra chairs around the table and put her boots up. I watched the way she stirred her coffee. It was hard to think that Sharon would be jealous of anyone.

—You know that can happen. I read about this woman who was a virgin when she married. On her wedding night, she was so mad for her husband she screwed up her back from fucking—and when she woke up the next day she was paralyzed from the neck down, Sharon grinned. She laced her fingers together and cracked her knuckles in my direction.

My skin felt hot and miserable.

—Sometimes it's like suffocating, I said.

—You know about snuff movies, don't you? she said.

Sharon explained about snuff movies and I tried not to believe her. I avoided her look, her smoke.

—I thought you'd been in love a million times, I said.

—Not really. I hate men, Sharon said.

I dug my fork into the chocolate torte. Love can make you so fat, so broke.

—Well? she said.

—What? I said.

—Did he recognize you, jerk? she asked. She reached over and took half the frosting off my dessert, starting at one corner, wrapping the fudge around her fork like fettuccini. She wasn't having anything to eat that day; she was dieting.

—I'm not sure, I said.

—What do you mean you're not sure? She stubbed out her cigar.

—I don't know. He didn't say and I didn't ask.

—Good for you, she said.

Then, as an afterthought, she said: As long as you're the one in control.

—But I'm not. That's what I'm trying to say. I'm completely out of control.

I watched her break off a large hunk of my cake and pop it in her mouth.

—But you slept with him? she smiled.

I don't know why, but all of a sudden I started telling her about the taxi. And once I did, it made me feel so crazy, I thought I was going to float right out of myself. I looked at the Alps to see if I could spot myself at some great altitude of madness.

—No one should have to go through life without doing it in a taxi. I feel so deprived.

—But I'm the one who was deprived, I said.

—In a really dramatic way. That has to count for something. Where did you find him, anyway? she asked.

—I can't say.

I looked at my watch—I didn't want to go into everything, his apartment, the balcony.

—What do you mean you can't say?

—I don't know. I have to go.

—Molly . . . , she said, taking hold of my arm.

—I guess you could say . . . I met him through my sister.

Sharon squinted at me. She rolled her tongue inside her lower lip and carefully weighed her sick notions of life against my giveaway expression. I rummaged in my purse for money as she sat back and laughed. Howled, really. The grumpy woman behind the counter, known for kicking out kids from our school, set her teeth into a hard cookie, waiting for the least provocation.

—I get it. He's one of your sister's castoffs, Sharon said.

Right away she knew how close to the bone she'd come.

—You shop your sister's hand-me-downs. You are bad, Molly. I absolutely love this. Does Amanda know? Or is she still seeing the guy?

I was having trouble finding enough money to pay for the torte Sharon had all but consumed.

—I'll have to call you . . . I'm really late.

—I told you, you're on the list already. The day is blown.

—No, I have to be downtown, I said, throwing on my sister's jacket.

—To see HIM?

—No, a gyno appointment, I grimaced.

—Beware the cold speculum, Sharon shouted after me, turning the bakery woman's face to liver.

Some people escape underground, some into a mind womb—a drug, any movie that's showing. I used to take the El. It's all the grit and funk of the world moving like it wants off its track. With every ride I could hear the screws coming undone, the scream of the wheels, the fall to the street. Most of us don't deserve all those turns we have to take, the ambulances, the media, the loss, the legend. . . . But it's thinking about all of us, being in that same condition, that can raise someone up in their purpose.

I escaped Sharon on the B train, tasting sky and soot, past the neighborhoods that change ethnicity like my sister changes purses. Into the world of doctors and lawyers and high finance. A place where people lose fortunes but can't leap from those high-rise windows because they're sealed shut.

Dr. William Sanders, OB GYN, was a dour man. He wasted no time putting equipment up me like he was filling a storage unit with his worldly possessions. Some doctors like to tell you every move they're making as if your body is a war game, others tell you grisly stories or cheerful anecdotes; Sanders said nothing. Before he was done, he took a second look at the questionnaire I had filled out. Then he gave me this look, considered my chart again and shook his head. He appeared to grin as if he knew something I didn't.

When he was finished, I worried that he'd left more inside me than his strange feelings on a chilly spring day.

The nurse said I could get dressed and the doctor would see me in his office.

Dr. Sanders's office had old leather chairs like the ones my father once had in his office. My father told me about the significance of chairs when seeing someone with psychological difficulties. He said a therapist will sometimes elevate or lower his own chair, to create a necessary effect. The unconscious desire to keep their backs from a door, like cardsharps sitting in a saloon, will cause some patients to gradually move their chairs across the room, leaving tracks in the carpet. He said some doctors invite the patient to select a chair at the beginning of a session—even the one normally taken by the doctor—to see how they're progressing. And though the effort to smash a doctor's chair was typically taken as a sign of aggression, placing one beyond the pale of normal social boundaries, my father had a case in which this bold stroke meant the fellow was no longer in need of therapy. My father shook his hand to wish him well, saw him to the door, and sent him a bill for a new chair. A much nicer chair than the one that had been destroyed.

That afternoon, I sat squarely on the arm of the chair Dr. Sanders offered opposite his desk. He pushed the chart in my direction and pressed the tips of his fingers together in expectation.

—Your father's name . . . it's a familiar one to me. I believe, and correct me if I'm wrong, that he was the psychologist who . . . ran off.

Dr. Sanders studied me, his eyebrows raised.

—How did you know? I said.

He showed me the space where I had written my father's name next to my mother's, as if they were adjoining gravesites. I guess it was something automatic, under the category of unconscious missteps. I didn't remember putting his name down, but there it was, in my handwriting.

—I read about your father at the time of his disappearance, he went on.

I hate doctors.

When I didn't cooperate, he took his tablet and wrote out the prescription for the birth control pill. He tore it off the pad and held it in his hand for a long time. His hands were red, probably from all the years of scrubbing, the use of latex gloves. Maybe he was allergic to his patients.

I tightened my eyes in his direction. My father's story had certainly aroused curiosity in strangers before; they were eager to talk once they found out I was his daughter. I always dreaded that moment. It wasn't uncommon for me to make up a different last name during the height of the media attention. I mean, a prominent psychologist vanishes without a trace, leaving his home, his family, a full appointment book. The investigation, the reporters. . . . Trying to explain or not explain was far worse than his leaving.

—I don't know what the odds are of you coming to me . . . with a whole city full of doctors, but. . . .

—My sister's secretary made the appointment. You'll have to ask her.

I opened my legs enough so he couldn't look at me without looking up my dress. It seemed like the right way to say "fuck you," at the time. And it did make him uncomfortable, funny as that was, considering his profession.

—No, I . . . you see, someone told me something about your father. A colleague of mine.

I didn't know where he was going and told him that. I could feel my stomach seizing up, my tongue drying out.

—What I'm trying to say is, I happen to be privy to certain information about your father's whereabouts. If I can rely on your strict confidentiality. . . .

—I don't understand, I said.

—Of course you don't. You couldn't. I just need to know that whatever I tell you stays in this room, he said, quietly tapping a pencil against his desk, eraser-end down.

—Kind of a role reversal, I said.

—If you will, he smiled awkwardly. Look . . . a colleague of mine was down in the Bahamas a couple of years after your father's disappearance, a fellow who might have belonged once to the same athletic club your father joined, Dr. Sanders said.

He put the prescription back down on his desk, just out of reach.

—This fellow saw your father go into a hotel there. My friend tried to catch up with him, but just missed your father going into an elevator. So he asked the desk clerk, and sure enough, your father was registered there under his own name.

My legs went slack and, though I tried to control it, my breath shortened. I managed to keep myself together enough to stand.

—I'm sorry. Can I get you a glass of water?

—I'm not thirsty.

I made a face at him, as if to say he should hurry and tell his story.

—My friend had to leave the next day and your father

wouldn't respond to his calls or messages. He thought about going to the police, once he was back in the States. But you know how it is. People are afraid to get involved. So he called your mother instead, figuring if she wanted to take it to the police it was her business. He said she was a little . . . odd over the phone. Didn't even want the name of the hotel. Not that I blame her. I mean if someone called me out of the blue like that. . . .

I knew what he was saying; I'd heard it before. My mother had been more of a patient to my father than a wife. Amanda had said things like that. I came around the side of the desk to snatch the prescription from his hand, but he held onto it for a few seconds. There was a silent tug-of-war before he let it go. He kept his eyes on me the whole time, no doubt trying to learn if I was more the daughter of the rebel father or the child of the crazy mother. I smiled at him and moved toward the door, stuffing the prescription into my purse.

I couldn't quite figure out what Dr. Sanders's game was; why the sadistic lingering over my troubles, until he said: You probably have no idea how many doctors envied your father.

I turned to look at him, to study *him* this time. I considered saying, "And did you envy his daughter?" but I didn't.

It was about vicarious pleasure; Dr. Sanders was patting my father's back right in front of me, with a large, collegial hand.

—I'm sorry. I can see I've overstepped my bounds.

Please take a seat; we should talk about STDs if you're going to be active. I just thought . . . if it was my father and someone knew something and didn't tell me. . . .

Since I'd already fished out my Lolita glasses from my purse, I put them on and, as I left, I said: Don't worry. I use my sunglasses for protection.

The last thing I wanted was to see Amanda, but I promised to stop by her office on the way home; she needed to talk about something. I was sure it was Nathaniel—there couldn't be anything else. I hardly saw her anymore; I kept my mess to the guest room; I wasn't going to flunk out or anything; I wasn't giving her much to complain about, really. And I didn't think she'd wait to tell me if Mom had died. But you never knew with Amanda. That was always there, the idea that my mother could actually die. I thought about it in everything I did and pushed it away every chance I got.

I stepped into the elevator of my sister's office building and looked at the long panel of buttons. The thought of Russian roulette went through my mind, where all the bullets—each floor—has a name on it, and you think it's going to stop at yours. Amanda worked on the twenty-second floor; the elevator car wasted no time getting there. I stepped out; black steel and sharp edges everywhere. I was about to take another elevator back down, when Edith spotted me. She said something to the receptionist and came over.

—She's expecting you, she said in her dry, Edith way.

My sister worked in a world of expensive chairs too pinched to sit on; phones that rang so often they seemed to be set on timers like church bells; tables stacked with photos, magazine clippings, layouts; coffeemakers always running empty, time running out, computers humming.

Edith dogged me to my sister's office. She wore a pale silk dress that day, with perspiration marks in prim yellow circles under her arms. Edith was older than the other secretaries and therefore no competition to Amanda. Balanced in her hand were papers, and mail, and what I figured was a gift from someone who wanted their product promoted in the magazine. She looked as if she wanted one central place to deposit everything—her entire, miserable work life.

I sat opposite my sister's desk and put my feet up. Edith studied me with pity. Her face lamented the fray at the hem of my dress, the wear on my heels, the bruise on my knee, the hair. God, the hair.

—Did she tell you why she wanted to talk with you? Edith asked in a whisper.

—Yes, she did, I whispered back.

—Well, good, she said in a normal tone. She went around to my sister's side of the desk and carefully arranged the items she had brought with her. Then she lined up the files and papers already there and wiped a line of dust away with one finger.

—I happen to think your sister's a saint. You have no idea how hard she works. Confidentially, I worry about her, Edith said. The circles under her arms grew.

It was easy to see how much she hated Amanda.

—A little . . . high-strung, I said, shaking my head.

—Anyone would be. With all the pressure. Especially with someone so young, she said.

—Have you ever been on the Pill, Edith?

Poor Edith never knew with me. She sat down in my sister's chair as if she could hardly stand any longer and sighed with grim purpose. I could see her trying to formulate some explanation about her age and menopause, the long absence of men. Maybe she was trying to think of the perfect phrase to enlighten me about the sensitive feelings and privacy of others. Or maybe she was working on a morals lesson, the threat of a well-deserved disease. Legends of syphilis passed down from her grandmother, what you purchased if you toyed with the bad side of fate.

But instead of sharing the least treasure, Edith said: My phone's ringing.

She held out an impatient hand and said: I'll take the prescription if you have it.

I fished it from my purse and handed it to her.

Once Edith had gone, I looked through my sister's desk, but I didn't find anything of any real interest. By the time Amanda walked in, I was rocking back and forth in her swivel chair, opening and closing her top desk drawer with one of my feet.

—If you find a sharp letter opener in there, I could use it, she said, slamming a file down on her desk.

—Hara-kiri?

She closed her door.

—I'm convinced every business has its little prick accountant with a Dumbo complex. Jesus Christ, the man wears me out. I'm going to have to work late tonight. Let's head over to the museum. We'll grab a quick sandwich at the deli on the way back and I'll send you home in a cab, she said.

Amanda's office was only three blocks from the Art Institute. I watched her dress flutter in the wind off the lake like a distress flag. She kept pulling at my sleeve, telling me to hurry. She was cold, she said, and didn't have a lot of time. I wasn't sure what the setup was, why we had to talk in the art museum, until we got there and I saw where she was taking me.

It was a little room, just past the central staircase. A room filled with Goyas. The bench she sat on faced a painting of a man in the middle of his own execution by firing squad, his arms flying up in perverse redemption. I realize that any metaphor can get too overbearing, but I was convinced Amanda had chosen this room with great care. My sister and her endless war. I watched as she tried to find a place to start.

Amanda claimed she felt useless in a conversation when there was trouble brewing. But I knew differently. It was all there, every word measured out, waiting on her tongue like hot candy. She knew exactly what she was going to say; she just had bad timing. Her thoughts rushed out ahead of her and the circumstances. All the unsafe, unkind words she thought she'd never have to use came spewing out.

My sister once told me I was the only person she could ever really talk to. I found that concept pretty scary.

I stood next to Goya's painting and flung my arms wide like the man about to be executed.

—I'm ready when you are, I said.

Amanda laughed.

—You know, I've been thinking, you should try out for a play. Your school has a pretty good theater department, she said, always eager to remind me of things that could build my résumé.

—Right, I said, making a face.

—Or maybe you'd like to be a copygirl over at the *Tribune.* I still have plenty of contacts there.

—That was *your* thing, thank you very much.

—You might enjoy it. And colleges like to see that you have some kind of practical experience, she said.

She had that look like she was climbing the ladder and no one could see up her dress. She was poised in midflight, her hair arranged just so around her face, nothing beat-in about her shoes or purse. Finances in order, career so on track it seemed to hover above the rails. All the rest in time, in her carefully orchestrated time. With that face that made you feel sorry for every moment you'd ever breathed, thinking you might have stolen some small amount of oxygen from her.

—Seriously, you should think about it, she said.

I sat down next to her, tucked one foot up under my bottom and let the other dangle. I glanced at the floor and discovered a pattern in the old parquet I'd never seen before, for all the years I'd walked the museum with Mother. After she finished blowing my cover, I planned to leave over that graceful floor and go find Nathaniel. She rested a hand on one of my shoulders, adding to the discomfort between us.

Maybe the air was too full of old executions; she still wasn't saying anything about why she needed to talk. Finally, I had to take things on myself.

—You've fallen in love with Nathaniel, haven't you? I said.

If we lived in my country, not hers, she would have asked me that question.

—Don't worry about that, she said. She smiled to herself.

—No? I said.

—I told you; I'm never getting married again.

—But if Nathaniel had come first. . . . I mean if you'd met him instead of Peter, you'd be married to him by now, wouldn't you?

She couldn't stand it when I brought up her first husband.

—You must lie awake at night making up these tortures. Hasn't anyone taught you about the inherent stupidity of trying to reinvent the past?

—What else can I do with my nights? They're so long, I smirked.

—Sleep, she said.

—Right. I know how much sleep you get.

—I had a dream about Nathaniel, she said.

—God, not one of your dreams, I said, pulling away.

—He was seeing someone else. A girl from . . . France.

—A girl from France, I repeated, my face still as a drawing.

Honest to God, there I was again, unsure of my own creation. I really couldn't tell if she'd found something out or if this was one of her fucking premonitions. Again, I looked at the man in the painting and wondered what it would be like to have bullets go through your body. Do you feel them right away or is the shock just too great for sensation? I mean, maybe by the time you realize the pain you're dead.

—I don't want to lose him, Molly. Especially right now, with *her* being in the hospice and everything.

She let her feelings float on the surface for a while, trying not to take on water.

I felt sick, convinced that everything was rigged. It was like being a contestant on one of those game shows from the Fifties.

—Have you asked him? I mean, if he's seeing someone else?

—He wouldn't tell me if he was.

—He wouldn't? I said.

—I'm too much of a realist. I have to live with the fact that he's the kind of guy who will . . . see others, who does, no matter what he says.

—So . . . there's nothing to worry about, right? I mean if he's not going to change and you've accepted that. . . .

—How old are you, wonder child? Look, it was just . . . the girl in the dream was different. I kept trying to talk with Nathaniel, and every time I'd get close to him, she'd push between us and start touching him right in front of me. Then a voice whispered that she was the face of the enemy. Or maybe it said: the face of my anima.

—Your animal?

—Anima. Never mind. But I'm convinced there is someone.

—So you're going to . . . ?

—I don't know, she said, looking at me as if she expected some kind of answer.

I had to remember at moments like this that Amanda and I were both trained by the same man. We had received the same lectures on strategy, on how to keep a poker face. Only she was older and must have absorbed things in a different way; probably retained more than I ever did.

One thing I knew, it was our father's way to "educate" with a parable, a story so loaded with meaning it was impossible to mistake.

I began to think about Amanda's dreams. Maybe they never even happened. Maybe they were just carefully designed inventions. A way to convey things she had no other way to express. I mean, other than to douse us all with lighter fluid and set the family ablaze.

This dream of hers could be her way of telling me she knew and to back off.

What was our father fond of saying? Play the game until you understand the game? You'll lose a few rounds, a few hands, but you'll win in the end.

—Start from the beginning. Tell me the dream again, I said.

—Why?

—Please, I begged.

—There's no point, she said.

—But that's the way they do it.

—Who does it? Speak sense, for Christ's sake.

—Well, our father for one. Remember? If we woke up with a bad dream, he'd make us tell it to him very slowly, and we weren't supposed to leave anything out, no matter how small. Then he'd tell us what it was really about.

—The baby of the family is going to analyze me now?

—Babies grow up and become terrifying adults, I said, coming as close as I could without exposing myself. I retreated into the other Goyas for a moment and waited for her move.

She chose to ignore my remark.

—Look, I need to get back. So just listen, okay? When I was in my junior year of high school, *she* sat me down in the living room, for this big serious talk, right? Do you have any idea what she wanted to talk to me about? French kissing. French kissing! She wanted me to promise I'd never French-kiss anyone. She didn't care about my career plans, where I was going to school. . . .

We both began to laugh. The guard whispered for us to keep our voices down. The great church of art. All that silence must offend the artists in their graves, I thought. Especially the big drinkers, the huge talkers.

—So you want me to promise the same thing? I said.

—I want you to tell me where you're going to college. I don't care where it is; I mean I don't care how much it costs. I'm going to see you get there—but you have to start getting your applications together. Alright?! she said, standing up as if all was settled.

—I didn't think there was any money left in the house, I said.

—God, she screwed up everything when she bought that miserable old house. But Edith is a whiz with figures and she'll help with financial aid forms and such and type your essays and we'll just do it. I make a decent living and we'll just make it happen. But you have to make a plan, alright?

—What if I don't want to go to college? I smiled, waiting to see her breath stop, her heart flatten out.

—And what if you never lose your virginity? she snapped, gathering her purse and jacket. We started back through the maze of the museum.

—You were born to torment me, she said.

I listened to the rhythm of her high heels, they echoed off a million cherished imitations of life. The Chinese exhibit, the Japanese, the gods of India.

—All I ask is that you find some place out of state. I won't pay for anything in state. It would be a big waste. Understand? You have to experience other places. I should have gone into an exchange program right from the beginning. You could go to Greece or France for a year! Italy, for God's sake. Italy. Look, I have to fly; I'll have to skip the sandwich today, she said.

She handed me enough money for three taxicabs home and told me she and Nathaniel would be in late. She wound herself up in the revolving door and fled down the long stairs.

I watched her for a long time as she tried to hail a taxi for the three blocks back to the office; Amanda hated the wind. She hated the least disturbance in the air.

EIGHT

I DIALED THE HOSPICE AND SOMEONE THERE WENT OFF to check on my mother, to see if she could talk. As I waited on hold, I thought of Amanda telling me, in the back of our father's car, to hold my breath when we passed a cemetery.

All the windows in my sister's apartment had been nailed down by the janitor that afternoon. The longer I held my breath, the longer I could avoid the stale exhaust from an entire winter trapped in Amanda's apartment.

I tried to imagine the hospice during the wait. The canned pea–colored walls, the person who turned my mother toward the phone, the tubes and packs that had to be adjusted, water offered with a stiff, bent straw to start her mouth, her thoughts.

Then all of a sudden she was on the phone.

—Mom?

—Yes, Molly, she said. It was as if we were sitting at the kitchen table together and I'd just turned to ask her the capital of Mississippi.

—Did I wake you? I said.

—No, I was just resting with my eyes closed.

—Mom . . . did Dad go to the Bahamas after he left?

—I don't . . . I'm not sure if I understand, she said, her voice trailing off.

—When Dad left us, did he go to the Bahamas for a while?

—I think you're a little mixed up, Molly. Your Dad and I honeymooned in the Bahamas. Funny you'd think of that.

—But a man didn't call you, a couple of years after Dad left, to say he'd seen Dad in a foreign country? I said.

—Are the Bahamas foreign? No, that doesn't sound right; your father wasn't much for traveling. Is there a reporter bothering you? It's such an old story; you'd think they'd have no interest in it anymore.

—No, Mom, there's no reporter. So you can't remember? At all? About a man calling?

—I think the medication . . . it makes me a little fuzzy sometimes.

—Amanda wants to send me away.

—I'm sorry. Wait, the nurse needs to talk to me for a minute. Just hold on, honey.

I wasn't sure if she was sorry that Amanda was sending me away or sorry that we were interrupted; maybe she was grateful. There was mumbling and then the worst sounds, my mother coughing, choking, groaning, the whine of the bed. I imagined the receiver being pressed into her chest, how she suffocated in sheets that felt hot and scratchy.

—Molly, I have to go; they want to give me a sponge bath. Was there something important you needed to talk about or can it wait?

—I need to come see you, I said.

—Maybe your sister will bring you out soon. Have her call me when she can. And don't worry about things, sweetheart.

Funny the way it is with some conversations. You know exactly what you're going to say and you know exactly what the other person is going to say and, in the end, you wish you hadn't called, but you did. You climbed right up on an old chair in your parents' house and let yourself swing from a telephone cord, in the high, thin air, not really caring if anyone cut you down right away or not.

As soon as my mind was pulled back into my sister's apartment, pried from my mother's feeble arms, I found a hammer in the kitchen.

I went through the whole place pulling nails out of window frames. The snow had disappeared from the ledges, only small blackened patches clustered in the park below and around a couple of cars that hadn't moved all winter. The janitor had turned down the furnace already; it didn't take long for the apartment to feel cool enough to preserve me.

I took a shower and turned on the three televisions. Then I put on every radio I could find—my sister had five in all. It was the news hour, and pretty soon I had a crowd of voices in the apartment, a regular gathering. For a while I tried to look at books, but Amanda got all of Mom's art books and that made me think about not getting any. I thought about food but the kitchen was in its usual barren temper. I considered love, but Nathaniel was coming over to see my sister.

When there was nothing left to do, I called the Hollister kid. I hoped he'd answer the phone because I was having the worst time remembering his first name. I took a chance on an M. N. Hollister in the directory, listed in the neighborhood where Sharon said he lived. I think I got a butler or something.

Hollister didn't seem to know who I was at first. When I mentioned Sharon, we both laughed. I wasn't sure why. Maybe it was just what people did when they thought about Sharon.

There were certainly reasons for asking a boy from my school over. Help with homework; a party because my sister was out of the house; the sound of a prowler and I just happened to see the class list with his name. Weak-suck reasons, but something to hang an invitation on. In the end, I didn't care about impressing what's-his-name Hollister. So I just asked him if he could come over and told him where I lived.

He said he'd be over in twenty minutes. I figured that meant forty. But the poor bastard was leaning on the bell in fifteen. I threw on one of my sister's kimonos, trembling in the cold air, and buzzed him in downstairs. It was hard not to think of Sharon's remarks about his lineage—the hair implants and lapdogs and all—as he climbed the stairs. I half expected him to show up with a manservant helping him slip into a dinner jacket.

But Hollister had dressed in such a hurry he had this inside-out appearance to him. And though I made an effort to find it, I was relieved that there wasn't anything too adult or productive in his expression. He had this sly, quizzical look. I could see why Sharon bothered to tease the guy.

Even if all I could do was think about Nathaniel.

—Quite a climb, he said.

—Have you heard the evening news? I said, suddenly conscious of the televisions and radios.

He stepped inside.

—We like to pay attention to the media around here.

—Okay . . . he smiled, a little doubtful, letting me take his jacket. I hung it in the closet next to Amanda's arsenal of coats and tennis rackets.

I showed him into the living room and asked him to take a seat. Then I went around the apartment and turned everything off.

With a brand-new pencil and fresh pad of paper from my sister's supply, I took a seat next to him. I had to keep pulling my kimono together.

—You didn't have to turn the news off for me, he offered.

—It's always the same, anyway. Don't you think? All those dead people out there. What would you like to drink?

—What do you have? he said and folded his arms over his chest. He looked cold.

—Anything. We have anything you'd like.

—Your folks home?

—I live with my sister. She won't be in till late, I said without smiling or giving much away.

The conversation turned to mixed drinks and we decided on margaritas. I showed him which cabinet the liquor had recently crawled into. He looked around and said we'd need margarita mix. I wrote that on the pad and said we should talk about what kind of food to get.

—Are you expecting more people? he said, showing his teeth in a nervous way.

—Not really. Do you want eggs? I feel like eggs, I said.

I wrote down eggs and English muffins and strawberry preserves. He said we should get some chips and salsa if we were going to bother with margaritas. I told him there was no point in ordering, really, if we didn't get some kind of dessert.

Then I asked if there was anything else he needed. Aspirin? Hand lotion? Magazines? Our neighborhood store was fully stocked, I said.

He declined with that same odd smile of his and stood up to look around. I put in an order at the grocery where my sister had opened an account. They told me it would be almost an hour before the delivery boy could make it over.

When I put the phone down, I came up behind my guest and said: You know, I can't remember your first name.

He laughed and told me, but a few minutes later I'd forgotten it again, maybe because I didn't use it right away. I started calling him Hollister and he didn't seem to mind.

—So, I'm curious why you asked me over, he said.

He had this way of sitting like he wasn't sure what to do with his legs. We were nursing old fudge jars of brandy, waiting for the margarita mix to show up. I studied him, looking for fatal flaws, signs of addiction, remorse, trauma. But he looked as if he was the kind of guy who was comfortable almost anywhere except in my sister's apartment.

—I don't know but I loved the way you just came over, I said.

He smiled as if he'd found something—maybe a mote; don't motes happen in eyes?

—You always like it this cold? he said, trying to be subtle about looking down my kimono.

The windows were so dark they were black, as if all the lights of the city had been extinguished. I wondered where Nathaniel was in the dark.

—The spring makes me crazy. Does it make you crazy? It's like I can't get enough air. It's always worse at night, I said.

He reached over and almost touched a strand of my hair, the way they do in romance magazines, but then he smiled and pulled his hand back.

—That's not your natural color, is it? he said. He looked embarrassed.

—It's hereditary. The whole family is prematurely platinum. So Sharon tells me you're going to be rich and famous, I said.

—Famous? No.

—I'd hate that, I said.

—You'd hate what? he said, taking the end of one of my kimono sashes without looking at it. He played with it like a tassel on a pillow; maybe he thought that's what it was, just a tassel to curl around his fingers.

—To know what things are going to be like; it's scary, I said.

—So you wouldn't want to be rich? he said, looking at me like I was in need of constant decoding.

—Not the way my sister does. She'd be in seizure heaven if she knew you were over here, sitting on one of her couches. She'd make me get out her real glasses, her crystal.

—But even if it wasn't about money, you just don't want to know what's going to happen, he said.

—People hypnotize themselves with the future. And if that doesn't work they pay people to go into trances or consult the stars. But things never turn out the way we anticipate. I mean, why get started in the first place?

The doorbell rang. At first I thought the grocery boy made it over super fast, but then it rang two more times. Amanda's signal—the one she used to let me know she was home.

I grabbed the brandy and pulled Hollister into the guest room. The door didn't have a lock, so we moved the desk in front of it. Then we sat on the spare bed in the dark. Amanda and Nathaniel entered the apartment. She came right over to the guest-room door and turned the handle. When her hand met my natural resistance, she said: Molly? You all right?

—I'm asleep, I shouted.

—We'll be quiet. Sorry to wake you, she said.

Hollister and I sat breathing for the longest time, listening to Amanda's complaints about the cold and spiders, which were intended for me.

I think it was Nathaniel who went around the apartment closing windows. I tried to look for him through the keyhole but all I saw was the quick streak of a dark coat. The coat I wanted to bury myself in.

Hollister waited in silence. Mr. Agreeable. It was our age, I guess. We were used to hiding out, sneaking, moving furniture in front of doors, sitting in the dark, just to make it through a week, a single day without being caught at things THEY did frequently and with relish.

I sat down next to Hollister again.

—We'll have to wait till things settle down before you can leave, I whispered.

Like a dream where you're suddenly naked in the wrong place at the wrong time, I saw that Amanda's kimono had come completely undone. My bare breasts were looking at Hollister in the dark.

As I pulled the silk together, Mr. Polite leaned back into the bed and took a peek out the curtains.

—This your room?

—Not really.

—Mind if I open the curtains?

—Just don't turn the lights on.

There was the strange angular view of the apartments across the way. On the top floor someone was watching TV in the dark, light moving against the ceiling. On the first floor, a woman was making dinner. She was always making dinner, no matter what time of day or night it was. Always in her flowered apron. Just for herself; no one came to eat her dinners. The scent of beef rose up through the hollow between the buildings. Hamburgers, steaks, stews, anything from a cow. *She* was a mean old cow, my sister said. Something about the shared parking lot in back and the abuse of assigned spaces.

—It's that second-floor apartment that gets me, I said.

I watched as his hands produced a joint from the thin air of his T-shirt.

—They refuse to open their shades. You see lights going on and off around the edges. You hear their TV and their radio . . . , I said.

—Big on the news? he said.

—Not like us.

I found a book of matches in the ashtray and explained that we had to fan the smoke out the window so my sister wouldn't use her little beagle nose and sniff us out.

—You never know if they're over there looking in your window. And you don't know if there's an old pervert who spills orange juice on himself or an overly dramatic actress who's going to leap from the window some night while you're looking that way or an ill child who can't move and wants to make contact, I said.

I told Hollister I hadn't smoked dope before, except

for a couple of times, and then I didn't really feel like I got high.

—You'll get high on this stuff, he said.

We smoked in silence and I listened for the smallest sounds from my sister's room. Though Hollister didn't understand that's what we were doing, he seemed to go along.

I just about fell off the bed when the doorbell rang. Hollister grabbed me and whispered with glee: The groceries.

We were both hungry and talked about storming the front door but instead we settled for listening to the conversation my sister had with the delivery boy.

—You must have the wrong address, my sister said into the intercom in the hall.

The tin voice of the delivery boy repeated the name and address. I imagined him shifting the groceries from one arm to another, restless, tired, ready to go home; surely this was his last delivery of the night.

Amanda walked over to the guest room and stood outside the door for a long time. Maybe she was about to roust me out, but for some reason decided against it. I think it had something to do with her endless desire to control the forces around her.

She returned to the intercom.

—No one orders groceries this time of night, my sister said in a bruising tone.

—The ice cream is going to melt, the delivery boy whimpered.

Hollister and I sniggered in the dark.

—You want to talk about melting? You have a woman here melting from a long, difficult day. We did not order any groceries and that should be the whole story.

—But what am I going to tell the manager?

—What are you going to tell the manager? You are going to tell the manager that I have a whopping bill from last month's overpriced groceries and if I say I didn't order anything, then the customer is always right. Got it?

There was no response from down below.

My sister stormed back into her bedroom. But I knew the way she operated. Next time that delivery boy came over she'd tip him three times the usual amount, invite him in to talk about his career plans, suggest there might be a decent gofer job for him down at the magazine.

I curled up into a pillow while Hollister kept guard at the window, sending the smoke out into the night. I would have given anything just then to hate Hollister, to think of him like a winter you get stuck in to the point of frostbite, even amputation. But I couldn't.

He played with my sash and hummed something so low I almost felt it in my bones.

—Shhh, I said.

—You look high, he said.

I covered my mouth so my sister wouldn't hear me laugh.

—Where's your bedroom? he asked.

For some reason I thought he meant my real bedroom. Because at that point, I still considered my room at Wharton Manor to be the only room I had.

—It's going to be torn down. The whole house is going to be torn down, I said.

—I'm sorry, he said, sounding perplexed.

—I'm not. I plan to travel, I said.

He said something about Hermann Hesse, something about wandering. I'm sure it was beautiful but it flew out the window in one quick gust, his hands directing everything into the ether between the buildings.

When the room suddenly lightened, I saw his face move toward mine.

I sat up and we almost knocked heads.

—What's that light?! I said.

—I don't know.

I pushed into Hollister's chest to steal his view and there was Amanda's reflection playing against our neighbor's dark windows. Her bedside light was on.

She either didn't care that our mystery neighbor could be watching or it added to her excitement. Or maybe she knew something I didn't—that the person in that apartment had died. She began to undress. Nathaniel undressed next to her, framed in the reflection of windows. I was watching a bad movie.

They were all over each other. I could see Nathaniel's hard-on, how he pulled her into bed. Then they were just out of view. I didn't even know I was crying like the spring coming loose from the winter until Hollister pulled me around to face him and touched my mouth.

I wanted to tell him he'd be a fool to do it with me.

But I said: Fuck me, Hollister.

And that's just what he did in the light from my sister's bedroom.

NINE

IF I HAD TO PINPOINT WHERE THE SUDDEN BALMY WIND came from that morning I would have said Las Vegas or some sleazy place in Florida. Maybe Hollywood. It was the first warm day of the year, but it felt like a cheap wind of little substance. I sat on the front steps to Nathaniel's apartment building, waiting for him to come home.

A drunk pulled up in a taxi, looking for the right steps to the right brownstone. His clothes were from last night, his face from years ago. There were people you knew were going to end up like that.

I don't understand living in a big city without a stoop to sit on. It's the only way to track humanity. There were three guys who lived down the street from Wharton Manor. The kind who'd steal your mail if they thought there was a government check inside. Sometimes my mother got unemployment checks; a few of them went missing. They'd purr if I went by in a summer dress. A couple of times they dragged our porch chairs down the street behind a car because it was such a hot day and there was nothing else to do. But those same guys wouldn't hesitate to protect you if anyone so much as breathed near your shoulders. One of them practically killed this guy who tried to rape a girl on our block once.

Amanda's building didn't even have front steps; she didn't know a soul for miles around.

I tried to think of what I'd say when Nathaniel came home, and what I'd say if Amanda was with him. I didn't come up with much because the whole thing made me too nervous. I was terrified to get thrown out of Amanda's, but I was just as scared to stay.

I watched a woman maneuver a stroller down the steps across the street. Her older child, a boy, kept kicking the fire hydrant near the curb, waiting for her. A nurse, who looked like she'd just gotten off work, stood looking at the mailboxes. Finally she opened one with a key and deposited that mail in her purse. She stood there for a long time, looking blank. Then she ascended wearily into her apartment building. The street got busy, deliveries were made, sounds crowded in and suddenly moved off. The sun kept angling up the steps and I had to keep inching into the shadows. Stoop-sitting is pure empathy. I don't think Amanda ever knew that.

There was the day she came down the manor stairs from Mom's room to let me know, for the first time, that someone from a hospice was coming to get my mother.

Amanda held an empty suitcase in her hands. She told me to fill it with enough clothes to wear for a time, an unspecified, involuntary amount of time.

I took the suitcase from her, went out to the front porch, and sat on the top step. That great sweep of stone. When she joined me outside, I said: I'm ready to go when you are.

My sister snapped her wedge-shaped shoes down the steps and tried to yank the suitcase from my hands. But they were completely slack, unable to hold a single thing anymore. The empty suitcase flew back and hit her in the lip, raising a bloody welt.

She cursed the egg that hatched me and ran into the house. A minute later, she ran back onto the porch with a cold compress. The sound of those violent shoes echoed down the street.

—You're truly her daughter, she said around the edges of her washcloth.

Her words were just red spit.

—You have to go upstairs and fill this goddamn suitcase with clothes if you expect to have anything to wear when you get to my apartment.

Then she softened, just a little, and said: I'll loan you what I can, Molly, but there *is* a limit.

I wasn't sure if she meant a limit to her wardrobe or a limit to her generosity. I suspected the latter.

—I might be doing some traveling and that thing is too heavy, I said. The suitcase gradually slid to the bottom step without anyone to resist its movement.

It was one of Dad's old suitcases that I hadn't seen for years. I wanted to ask if she'd stolen it from him or from Mom or just the house, but she was beyond the stage where it was a pleasure to piss her off.

When I thought I heard her in my bedroom, I followed her upstairs and stood in the hall and watched her for a while. She filled the suitcase like a washerwoman slapping clothes against a rock. T-shirts, pants, things she knew I didn't wear anymore, just to show me what my lack of co-operation would buy me. It took the addition of a leaking bottle of shampoo, a tube of toothpaste stuck to a hair-brush and an open container of baby powder—the fine talc shooting from the little holes on top—to settle her down. But then the talc flew into her open mouth and nose and Amanda's dramatic coughing and sneezing woke Mom.

I called to see if she wanted anything. I heard her turn over in her bed.

—Everything's fine, Molly.

I went back downstairs and sat on the front steps. I was going to wait for the night and the sounds of the distant train. It was too cold that day, but in the summers, every person with a step to sit on in that neighborhood was out melting with the last of their ice and warm Coca-Colas. It wasn't as if we really knew each other and shared recipes and gossiped about the married woman who was having an affair down the block. But we knew the stairs we occupied—never mind that the man who smiled at me across the way had yanked my mother's car radio once.

I was trying to conjure up every face that belonged to every step, and the faces of their children, and their grandchildren, as if I could believe in the survival of that place, when Amanda snuck up behind me, swinging the suitcase into my spine, saying it was time to say good-bye to Mom.

—I'm not the one sending her away. You say good-bye, I said, rubbing my back.

Amanda just stood there, as if her presence meant authority, order, influence.

—The driver from the hospice will be here any minute and no one's sending her away.

—They're coming to get her but no one's pitching her out. Right, I said.

—You'll feel terrible if you don't.

She sat down on the step beside me, freezing in her thin little sweater.

—You'll feel terrible the day you realize what you've done. We should take care of her here, I said.

—It's not like we haven't discussed this.

Amanda attempted to put her arm around me, which forced me to slide to the far end of the stair.

—You've discussed it with your ego, I said.

—I think you mean *id*. Look, Molly. Do you know how to change a catheter?

She knew medical things made me queasy. She just grinned.

—So you're going to take care of her and the house and

pay the mortgage and the utility bills and buy groceries and get through high school and. . . .

I didn't wait to hear about the business expenses also known as dinners out or how Amanda's credit cards were fueled by a city of impulse.

—We could take care of her at your place, I said.

—One of us happens to have more than a full-time career, Molly, which means entertaining people at my place on occasion. And where would you sleep if I gave her the guest room? For Christ's sake, she needs a lot more care than either of us could ever provide. Medical care. And . . . you know she and I can't stop fighting and that would only make her condition worse. She needs to rest.

Sometimes I felt my sister was something you could fill to the very top, and still there was little to see when you looked inside.

—You mean she needs to die because you can't stop being such a bitch to her?

The air felt thick, the light brash and slow to move off. I kept thinking that after Amanda was done, Wharton Manor would be only an impression, less than solid memory. She'd quickly settle down to a real talk with her developer friend. She'd want to show me plans, the ghostly imprint of progress drawn up in blue lines. She was warming up the wrecking ball.

—I just wish . . . , she said, as the first of her tears rushed down her face, her makeup still unmolested. I just wish you'd tell me why you hate me so much, she said.

She knew why. Everyone knew why. If she got me to say it, she'd have something to resist, or strike out at, or maneuver away from. It was better if it remained the unspoken, unnamed thing between us—the poison fruit on a table where both of our chairs were drawn up, our stomachs empty. Because that was our game. Maybe not the game our father intended for us, but the one he helped set up in us nonetheless.

So I left her shivering on the steps, the cold adding to the grief she was willing to display for the neighbors that day.

I went back upstairs.

Since her illness, Mom had taken to draping old towels over every chair she sat in, as if a contagious fluid might escape her body and destroy the fabric. I don't think she understood that Amanda would simply have a thrift store come out and haul those chairs away, along with the rest of the furniture, the bedding, the glasses. . . .

I found her propped up in the easy chair in her bedroom, surrounded by the garish fish and suns of old beach days. I knew it had taken a real effort to get there. The light from the floor lamp angled across her face in such a way, it almost looked as if she intended to get a tan in the bedroom where I had never known her to fully open the curtains.

I turned off the lamp. I think the sudden darkness made her start. It was as if I'd turned off an old movie in which she was so lost she had become the heroine. There was a soft, moving edge to the objects in the room now; they were living, breathing things that I could never appreciate in the light.

—Are you all right, dear? she said.

I sat across from her at the foot of the bed.

—Amanda will bring you out very soon and we'll have a long visit, she said.

Then she laughed and said: We'll probably see more of each other there than we do at home.

I could hear the difficulty in her breathing. True air was something she'd never really have again, to hold safe and quiet in her chest. Yes, we'd have our visit, in a miserable park on the North Shore where she'd try to give me back everything I had ever given her.

I got up and went over to her dresser. There were the perfumes she'd once purchased to please my father, turned to alcohol long ago. I touched the bottles and brushes and little jars as if I was blind and needed to find one particular thing—something my hands couldn't quite remember.

—You know I never was much for jewelry. But there's a ring that was your grandmother's, a small emerald.

—Amanda can have it, I said.

—That's what you've said about everything, Molly; Amanda can have it. She has more than enough. There must be something you want for yourself.

It's funny about leaving some places. I imagine it's like death—when your life parades in front of you in detail. I could see every last item that house possessed, from my mother's photo album where half the pictures had people cut out or disturbed in some way, to the hats my sister collected up in her closet but seldom wore (unaware they had become small hatcheries for spiders). Bent silverware, rubber boots and snow shovels, the drawer for the silver foil with too many loose utensils always making it difficult to put the box back after you tore off a sheet of foil. . . .

I had three large dressers in my room and they were all full of stuff and my closet was bursting, my bookshelf crammed full. But I really didn't want any of it anymore. I'd outgrown things or lost interest in them or just couldn't imagine the process of going through and figuring out what was worth keeping—what I might want someday when I had my own place. And besides, no one seemed capable of telling me where I'd store stuff till that day.

And there were all of Mr. Graf's possessions. But no one ever discussed the back of the house where he had rented our rooms. In fact, no one brought him up at all.

It made me sick to think of Mr. Graf. Especially on a morning when I was looking forward to seeing Nathaniel. So I was relieved when some guy interrupted my reverie to get out of Nathaniel's building; I was blocking the door.

A sleek pair of legs in little running shorts, he had bright shoes and thick socks and apologized too many times for making me move all of two feet along the step. I kept thinking this guy is too nice for his own good; no one can survive like that.

—You waiting for someone? he asked, putting one of his shoes up on the railing and stretching his muscles out. He had a funny, square face like a cereal box and a healed-over broken nose that made me think of Peter, Amanda's ex-husband.

—Mmm, yeah, I said.

—Nathaniel, I bet.

There was a look like *all* the women wait for Nathaniel, early in the morning, on the front steps of his building.

—Expecting him back soon?

—Sort of, I said.

He laughed and tightened his buns.

—Well, I'll see you, he said, and took off down the block.

Forty-five minutes later, when the runner came back, sweaty and high, he didn't seem surprised to see me there.

—Hasn't come home yet, mmm?

—It's still early, I said and shifted into the last of the shade.

—You're welcome to wait for him at my place while I shower up.

—I . . . probably shouldn't, I said.

—Or use my phone to call him.

—Maybe. I'll think about it.

—I've got fresh bagels, coffee. Hey, I've even got strawberries.

I do love strawberries. And he seemed harmless enough. His apartment was across the hall from Nathaniel's.

Right away he got out this massive bowl of strawberries that looked like they'd been flown in from California that day with the sun still clinging to them. He put the bowl on the bar between his small kitchen and the living room—it was the same layout as Nathaniel's, only in reverse. I sat on one of the stools and watched him and listened for Nathaniel.

He toasted up a plate of bagels, made coffee, filled a cream pitcher and put out three kinds of preserves in little crystal dishes. He placed a slab of cream cheese on a plate with a special kind of blunt knife.

While he took his shower, I ate most of his strawberries. When he came back he was in a different pair of running shorts. No shoes, bare chest, hair towel-dried and fluffed up as if he had no intention of combing it.

—No sign of him?

—If you have to be somewhere . . . , I said.

—I'm not on till this afternoon. Relax.

—Are you a chef? I asked.

—I'll take the compliment, thank you. But I'm a swim instructor.

He did have a perfectly molded, waxy body. I recalled that one time, when Sharon was talking about us going to her parents' country club, she went on about the competitive swimmers that practiced in the pool there. She planned to make it with at least a half-dozen serious swimmers before she died; she figured it would be like making it with dolphins. She said there are women who do it with dolphins. And then, of course, she had to get into a whole thing about bestiality. In any case, swimmers shave their entire bodies from head to toe so they can move through the water like sea creatures.

He told me he swam competitively.

—You shave your legs?

—Legs, arms, chest, back. You get used to it.

It was strange to think that this smooth stone of a boy was actually hairy. I'd never met a guy that needed to shave his back before, under any circumstances.

—I love to swim, I said.

—You'll have to come to the pool where I work. It's pretty dreamy. Do you swim much?

—Not really. But I have swimming dreams, I said.

He looked at me as if I might be concealing fins.

—Wish I did, he smiled.

—Sometimes I think that's how I'm going to go; drowning.

—You're too young to have such dreary thoughts, he said.

—People always say I look younger than I am, I said.

He smiled and looked at his near-empty strawberry dish.

—You in school? he asked.

—No . . . I work at a magazine.

When I gave him the name of Amanda's publication he told me he read it all the time. He dragged out an issue from the bottom shelf of his coffee table.

—You listed in the credits? he said.

—Sure.

I took the magazine from him and rested it in my lap for a moment. Asked him if he knew Nathaniel very well.

—Not really. We keep different hours.

I found Amanda's name and returned the magazine to him, pointing to the listing.

—Lifestyles editor. How does one get to be a lifestyles editor?

—It's a long story, I said, accepting another cup of coffee. I can't believe Nathaniel isn't here yet. We were supposed to get out for an early game of tennis, I said, looking up at the wall clock.

—Friendship or rivalry?

—Something more dangerous, I said.

He smiled again but didn't ask. Unlike Sharon, however, I didn't want to make it with a dolphin.

—You know I have a theory about water.

—And that is? he said.

—Well . . . the city was destroyed by fire once, right? And most of the big cataclysms seem to be about fire or water. So I think the city's going to be destroyed by water next time. Everything floating through the streets and out into the lake. Millions of computers and desk chairs, billions of boxes of pencils and coffeemakers. Think of how many high-rise office buildings there are downtown. Think of all the stuff inside them.

My sober swimmer and I had a laugh. When we were quiet again, the room began to suck air looking for the slightest movement, any breath or thought between us. He finally went over to the balcony, to open up the door and let a breeze through. We both heard the elevator kick into gear and stop on his floor.

He started to say something but I shushed him, wondering how a swim instructor could be so insensitive to the moment. I ran over to the peephole. There was Nathaniel brooding in his leather jacket. Just as I had my hand on the knob, ready to open the door, Amanda came into view. She wore this bright turquoise dress that called unnecessary attention to her legs. Amanda, who never knows how to let someone brood in peace, pulled on Nathaniel's arm so he had to stop what he was doing and kiss her. It was a dreadful, do-I-really-have-to-do-this kind of kiss that made my spine hot. Then he had the door open and they were gone, inside his apartment.

I looked back at the pathetic swimmer. He bobbed in the fluid that filled my eyes.

—You okay? he asked.

—I just realized it's the wrong Saturday. We're supposed to play tennis next week. It's impossible to keep track anymore. I'm totally overworked.

—I can't imagine the stress of putting a magazine together. You do a fantastic job.

I hated his gratuitous, smooth little self. It was such a nothing publication. Just a set of glossy photographs and self-important articles. Everything a little too clever, a little too showy. Pumped up with questionable advertising—things you could never feel morally pleased about—cigarette ads, bourbon ads. I mean who drinks bourbon? Old men probably. Rich old men.

—It's crap, really. I suppose you don't smoke, I said.

—Sorry.

I lay down on his perfectly white couch and put my old boots up on the armrest. I saw him flinch. I guess the couch was new or something; he saw me as a potential stain. But I knew he wouldn't say anything. He was too busy driving through fantasyland, his arm out the window, sleeve fluttering, my mouth on his dick, my head just grazing his steering wheel. You'd wear yourself out if you thought you had to grant every guy's salty wish in this life.

Maybe I hoped Nathaniel would hear us next door. He'd recognize this lost sound coming from my throat and realize he'd better find it and hold onto it before it's too late.

—I broke up with the only man I ever loved this week, I said.

He said something about me being a little messed up with his eyes. And I said something about him having water on the brain with mine.

I got up and tromped to his shower. I knew it was in that

place just opposite Nathaniel's. I used his big, foamy bar of soap and his tender, giant towels.

—Sorry for eating most of the strawberries, I said, when I came back into the living room, combing the water out of my hair.

Then the idea came to me. The one I should have had right from the start when I was looking through the peephole. It would have been a lot cleaner if I had, but you can't plan everything out.

I explained to him that I had an old, dear friend—someone he might like to meet in fact, an avid snorkeler actually—and that she and I had been playing practical jokes on each other for years.

I really don't know why he cooperated; maybe it was the quickest way to get rid of me. I popped a bit of bagel with cream cheese and preserves into his mouth and rang Edith's number. He went into the bedroom and I listened in on the other phone.

He told Edith he had just moved into the apartment beneath my sister's. The pipe must have burst upstairs. There was water everywhere! Edith was listed as the person to call if my sister couldn't be reached in an emergency.

I'm sure the swimmer was having fun with this one, because the name I gave him for the apartment owner was the name I claimed as my own—we were all Amanda to him. His call came out more garbled than I would have liked and went on a bit long. But I knew what would happen the minute they hung up. Edith would start calling around for Amanda. After there was no answer at the office, she'd try Nathaniel's.

The swimmer returned to the kitchen to clean up. I slipped into my clothes and waited.

It's hard to describe the glory of hearing Nathaniel's phone ring as I moved toward the open sliding door. The mighty satisfaction of hearing his front door open. Running back to the peephole, I caught Amanda's turquoise butt flying down the hall toward the elevator.

The sad reality of it—sad for my sister anyway—was that Nathaniel was not the kind of guy who would chase after her plumbing. He wouldn't be the one to bail her out or even stand outside her building, catching things as they flooded out her windows to the street below.

He remained behind.

I went into the kitchenette where the dolphin boy was busy loading his dishwasher. He looked troubled, unclear about events, like he was getting desperate to get a clean shave and go for a long swim.

—I wrote down your number, I said.

I took the elevator down to the first floor, got off and waited a couple of minutes, just to shift gears. Then I called the car back and returned to Nathaniel's floor. In this way I was able to arrive at his door as a fresh person, newly made, undamaged by all the days that came before, unformed by the nights, created out of ether and peroxide. Yvonne. The simple island of Yvonne.

But Nathaniel didn't see the simplicity of the moment. I could tell when he opened the door. I followed him inside instead of saying I'd come back at a better time, which I should have.

—Which cloud did you drop from? he asked. He went into his kitchen and got the bottle of cold vodka from the refrigerator; he poured one straight up and held the bottle in the air as an invitation. I looked past him and pointed to the one Coke trying to hide on the bottom shelf. He threw the can across the room and it hurt my hands, but I caught it without complaint.

—What's wrong? I said, dropping into an armchair.

—Other than life in general? he said, watching the lake. The glimmer and void of the lake where I was certain Amanda's dress still bobbed from our night on the balcony.

I picked up the can of soda and teased the pop-top with my fingers.

Nathaniel went over to his wall of music. He ran his fingers along CD boxes, as if he were the arm in a jukebox, set in motion by so many bad stories, a large number of them his own. He put on some jazz and sat down in the easy chair across from me. We both put our feet up on the coffee table. I imagined the glass breaking from the weight of our boots.

—You don't drink much, do you?

—No, but I smoke, I said.

Nathaniel reached into his shirt pocket, pulled out a pack of cigarettes and shot them across the table. The matches were tucked inside the cellophane. Smoking was a habit I'd been trying to acquire for some time. He held out his hands so I'd throw the pack back, but instead I lit a new cigarette from the one I held. I wanted him to see the film-noir life we could have together. But I dropped one of the two lit cigarettes and had to retrieve it from under the couch before it burned up his carpet.

He told me to just throw the pack. I hated the flatness in his voice. I wanted to shut his eyes and climb on top of him and change the winds hammering against his brain. But I was sure he'd push me away.

—How old are you? he asked, swirling his drink.

—No one's sure; the records were destroyed, I said.

—You're younger than you let on, I know that.

—Maybe I'm older, I said.

He went back to the refrigerator, got his bottle of vodka and set it on the coffee table. He laughed to himself.

—I bet you think your personality's still forming, as if there's some factory of raw material to work with out there. As if there's all the time you could ever want.

—I think the factory went on strike a long time ago, I said.

—That's right. On strike. I forgot you're the clever one.

—The clever one what? I said.

—Just the clever one, he smiled, and leaned back in his chair. Maybe he thought he could really see me through his bottle of cold vodka, like I couldn't see myself. And maybe he knew from the first, when he saw my platinum hair glowing in the taxi outside his apartment, that I was Amanda's sister.

—My girlfriend's giving me an ultimatum, he laughed again.

I guess we all kept him pretty well amused.

—I hope you don't think I'm your girlfriend.

I went into the kitchen to see if I could line up a glass and some ice.

—No . . . you're more like a fog that shows up every time I hit a curve.

—So I make you want to slow down, I said, trying to understand why no one I've ever loved could keep an ice cube tray filled.

—Not exactly, clever one.

I hated the way he said the words "clever one." And I hated Amanda for pushing him into such a state. I knew I should have left, but I finally forced open the Coke without much explosion and said glibly: So she wants to get married all of a sudden.

—You're spooky. That's right. She wants to get married. Just this morning she said: "Two weeks; married or get lost."

I was amazed and not amazed. Like watching a magician; the eye is dazzled but the mind is confident that simple tricks are being executed; nothing you couldn't do yourself with enough practice, the right equipment. I thought someone would have to talk her into getting married again; not the other way around. I looked at Nathaniel's troubled face and made a real effort to stay on track.

—You can get mighty lost in two weeks if you want, you know, I said.

—You can get just as lost getting married. It almost doesn't matter. Time is the real lie. You'll see, he said.

—So what are you going to do? I said.

—What do you want me to do? he said.

There's no way I could understand what he meant by that—not in the state he was in, not in the state I was in. But for the longest while I would drive myself mad thinking he had asked me to decide for him and that I didn't. I could have told him how to say good-bye to Amanda—even made him feel he was doing something noble. It was, however, just as likely that all he wanted me to do was wrap him in another bright fog and smash up his motorcycle for him. If there are pivotal moments, I'm sure that's when I landed in one; I just couldn't see it at the time.

What I did know, or thought I knew, was that Amanda didn't really want him, not for keeps. I was convinced she was just in one of her desperate moods. In a couple of months things would turn sour, and she'd be beating herself up for wasting her time on him. The funny thing was, I thought he and I had a better chance of making it, if anyone did. It should have been obvious.

Finally, I decided I better stop breathing life into Amanda, raising her up to a purpose when we were all so busy falling.

I went into his bedroom and found his ties. I took off my clothes and began to blindfold myself. It made me pretty queasy. Doing it myself was like pushing a wet hand toward a light socket. But even with the shakes, it was that kind of sensation that makes you feel . . . engaged; it's hard to explain. It was a state so completely in the present.

I walked out to the living room and stood there waiting. I heard Nathaniel get up and go into the kitchen. The refrigerator door opened and I heard him rummage around, moving jars and bottles over the grates of the shelves. I thought of Sharon's introduction to the world of food sex—the boy she told me she met in Paris, the pesto sauce he smeared on her skin until she was something from the jungle, naive like a Rousseau painting. I thought of other foods—creams and fruits and sauces.

The refrigerator door slammed shut. I felt the air as he went past me; I think he put on his jacket. The apartment door opened. He probably went out for booze.

I didn't take my blindfold off. I just stumbled over to one of the easy chairs and sat down, waiting for him to come back. Waiting against the silk of Nathaniel's tie. Waiting as I used to wait with Amanda, for my turn at the tray. My skin on fire. Waiting to beat him at the game.

The way Amanda did once.

Most of the items on the tray that day were ordinary things, a spoon, a pen, a hairbrush. My father loved to trick us by providing a good quantity of such everyday items, so there was little to call attention to any one thing. But on that particular day, he added to the tray a girl made of china.

She wore a white pinafore over a blue dress and held a teapot by the handle. She was all of an inch-and-a-half high and very important to me, since I'd won her at a party at school. I kept her in my top dresser drawer in a box with tissue. Seeing her like that, prone on his silver tray, I was angry that he had rummaged in my things that way. But I was also relieved that I would know at least one of the objects on the tray without fail.

In a matter of seconds, the smooth cloth descended on the tray and our father began the game.

—Alright, Molly. You can start, he said.

This meant my sister was to remain absolutely expressionless and silent, waiting for me to complete my list before she attempted hers.

I smiled into the great, soft eyes of my father as if we were coconspirators, and breathed in the scent of the pipe tobacco in his room.

—Well . . . there's a little china doll with a white pinafore and a blue dress holding a teapot and there's. . . .

Before I had a chance to go on to the next item, he said: Sorry, that's wrong, Molly.

—But it's right there, I said, pointing to the place over the cloth where I knew it rested on the tray.

I looked to my sister for help. Her breath and her face and her heart were like the stones on my father's desk, only more silent. Because even those stones had messages, since they were petroglyphs. My sister refused to give me the slightest signal, to help me in any way.

—You took it from my bedroom and you put in on the tray, I said to him bravely.

—I saw you with your little china doll just this morning at breakfast. You've mixed everything up in your head. It isn't here, he insisted.

He went on about the dangers of a vivid imagination, cautioning that this was the very thing that had gotten my mother into such trouble. To prove his point, he broke one of his own rules. He took the cloth from the tray to show me that the china figure wasn't there. And it wasn't. It wasn't there at all. He wouldn't even allow me a chance to feel the shock—that my doll had somehow vanished. He told me I had hypnotized myself into believing it was there. I watched him return the cloth to the tray.

Now my sister had had a full minute to study the tray. He asked her to name everything she had seen. Amanda took her time, slowly going over the everyday items he had placed there with care. She named things I hadn't seen at all, but then she'd been doing this game with my father forever. She seemed to come to the end of the list and my father said: Is that all?

—No. There's a small doll made of china wearing a blue dress and a white pinafore. She's holding a teapot by its handle, Amanda said. I studied the faint sliver of a smile.

—How is it possible your mother has raised two such idiots, my father said, going over to his desk and filling his pipe.

—You palmed it, Amanda said.

My father flew into a sudden rage and threw his pipe, one of his favorites, against his desk breaking it in two. He told her to get out of his study; he never wanted to see her again.

But Amanda said he didn't intimidate her. She was going to stay until she searched every corner of my father's study for that little china figure.

He told her she was grounded, that she wouldn't be able to leave the house for a month. He said this as he retrieved the two halves of the pipe and tried to force them together without anything to bind them. I began to cry because I knew my sister would never be able to take such confinement.

She said: I don't give a shit. That doll is in this room and you can go to fucking hell, Mister Psychologist.

My father began to laugh, in a huge way like a pot making soup out of a large piece of meat. He came round the desk suddenly and took my sister's wrist and twisted it until it burned; I knew this from the expression she made and the mark he left. But she didn't let out a whimper. Then he reached in his pocket, dropped the china doll into her palm and let her go.

—And now who do you think is going to succeed in life? Who do you think will possibly know how to succeed? he roared.

He swung around and looked at my face, covered in snotty tears and said: You let me hypnotize you, didn't you?

Before I could answer, he went into a long dissertation about how we had allowed ourselves to be hypnotized into a miserable set of ill-gotten beliefs. We were just three-foot-high dolls—small mirrors reflecting the emptiness of our time. We were obsessed with the material, he said, lost in the false promises of wealth and status. He said people would submit to almost anything now.

The rest of it's gone. Like the china doll that disappeared that day. My sister claimed she didn't know what happened to it, didn't care. And I would never bring it up with my father. Mercifully, it was the last time we had to play guess-the-objects-on-the-tray. There were other games with higher stakes. And then he left. The silver tray that seemed as big as a small lake, the blindfolds and metal bowls that made music when struck, the spinning wheels—those strange objects I often wondered about—none of those things ever showed up again.

As far as I was concerned, he could spend the rest of his days conjuring up his spiteful self, a man coaxing his own poisonous snake from a basket. But Amanda always worried me, the way she relished her role as silent traitor—and that feeling I was left with, that I knew what must be done with a traitor in the end.

It was such a sad little war. A scratchy piece of footage from an unpopular film. She should have let me in on it; come to my rescue; returned the doll to me. But that's the way it was with Amanda. Everything got in the way until I couldn't see straight when I was around her. Because when I think about it now, at least she told him to go to hell.

I sat shaking in Nathaniel's chair. There was no purpose to any of it, I kept thinking. No purpose at all.

I wanted, in moments like that, to flee to my mother or the things that were like my mother. To go lose myself in the cool marble of the Art Institute. It was the one most valuable thing she had been capable of teaching me. That the paintings really can drift from their walls and enclose you to such a degree, you become oil and canvas and color, even sense of place, however abstract that place may be. That few things outside of that feeling ever really matter. I had my hand up to take off the blindfold when I heard the elevator.

Someone got off on Nathaniel's floor. I kept the blindfold in place and waited for my stranger, listening to his footsteps in the hall. I think that's what most of us want—the chance to make it with a total stranger—without the worry over what they're about or what they can't live without. I think it's the only way we become strangers ourselves, free of ourselves.

I guess he hadn't bothered to lock the door, so I didn't hear the key. In fact, as far as I could tell it was left open, so anyone coming by the apartment would see me there. I heard his clothes drop to the floor, but I didn't hear his leather jacket, his boots. It sounded like someone else's clothes. Lighter or maybe heavier, I wasn't sure. When he pushed his dick into my mouth that fast, I wasn't sure if he really tasted like Nathaniel. I began to think he was a different man. Maybe the janitor or the delivery boy. He could have sold magazines or candy bars for a local charity. He could have been there to renew insurance, to break down the differences between term and whole life. Someone could have phoned with a desperate need to confide in a pastor and the pastor wandered into the wrong apartment, the wrong mouth. I could have been squandering some poor boy's virginity or arousing the last passions of a drifting man. Nathaniel might have sent a friend up to his apartment, a business associate or a guy from down at the neighborhood bar; I wouldn't put it past him.

He saved nothing for me. But maybe there was nothing left to save. More than anything, I wanted to get out into the air. I stumbled into the bedroom and found my clothes and dressed, unwilling to remove the blindfold until I got into the hall. He didn't say a thing, only touched my hand for a brief moment, trying to transfer some warmth or discover if I had any left. I was in the elevator and gone.

TEN

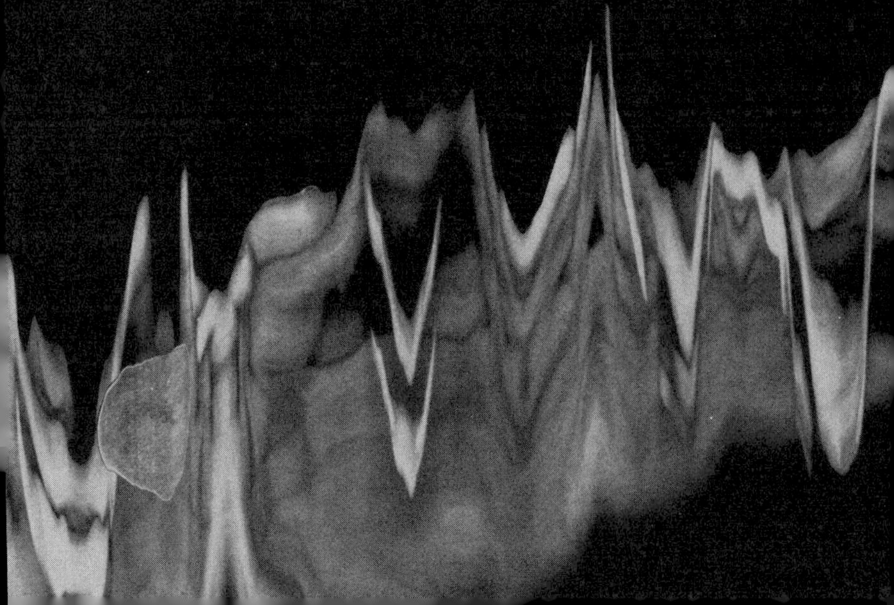

HOLLISTER DROVE ME THROUGH THE NORTH SHORE TO the old house. I don't mean Wharton Manor. But the house before that—the one that was so light and available to the world.

Its white columns had been like capped teeth set in the massive porch. It was the last prop. The last effort at facade that my father purchased for my mother in the hope of elevating her spirits, or so Amanda said.

But the doors were never flung wide. The wisteria, planted to lace around the columns and through the trelliswork, developed some kind of rot. The callers, who might have driven up with cakes and pies and baskets of good cheer, kept their distance. Although my celebrated father was discussed at their luncheons down the block as if he were more magazine article than man, it was decided, for mysterious reasons, that my mother would be a bad influence on their children. Amanda told me this, and that shortly after we moved in, our mother began to put on weight, in modest additions at first, gradually becoming a great dwelling of a woman.

Maybe that was what kept her from furnishing the house. Of course she was the kind of Depression child who was too quick to see extravagance in the purchase of a tea table, excess in a lounge chair, the fall of civilization in an Oriental rug. Despite this, Amanda managed to decorate the living room, and her bedroom with its adjoining bath. She had this docent way of directing her friends to one of those three locations, so that for all intents and purposes, the house had that normal, affluent feel.

The temperature dropped the minute Hollister's car rode into that rarified atmosphere, as if it was suddenly trying to shift back to winter. I cranked down my window, and stuck my arm out, checking for childhood conditions in the dark. There were plenty of stores and shops I didn't recognize. The Woolworth's was gone; it had been the only real place for miles. Signs were tacked everywhere about Dutch elm disease, entire neighborhoods losing their trees. It was hard to believe that blight could occur where the citizens kept such careful controls on their environment.

In a way I was relieved when we finally arrived and saw, under the influence of strong streetlights, that the old homestead was shrunken. Maybe it was the dominant line of the fence surrounding the property now, all that wrought iron taken to a ridiculous height. I imagined the owners liked to impale the heads of thieves, alley cats, and former residents on the topmost spears. Amanda told me the house had been purchased by the president of a large paint company, which was odd because the entire house was painted white. There's a kids' book in which kittens dump cans of paint over everything, color everywhere, blending and making new colors. That was my first impulse, to buy paint—made by the owner himself—and throw it at his pristine house. But it was too late at night, the stores would be closed, and it was probably all for the best because I had to stay focused.

—You don't happen to have a shovel in your useless little Fiat? I said.

Hollister cut the engine.

—What do you have in mind? he grinned.

—We need to get in that backyard and we need something to dig things up.

—I'm sure they have shovels. Maybe even a lawn mower. A little midnight mow? he said.

—Come on, Hollister, I said, opening my door.

—Are we digging up a family pet or an old uncle? he asked.

—Lies. We're digging up old lies, Hollister.

He nodded as if he understood. It's like that when you've

been raised by alcoholics; nothing seems to faze you. I bet his family had enough lies buried in their backyard to start a bone farm.

I tried, at first, to squeeze between the open bars of the fence and finally gave up and let Hollister go to work. He had us up and over that fence in a matter of seconds. It's funny with rich kids. They learn pretty early how to break and enter, how to steal in a guiltless way. To pinch things from their folks' country clubs or slip on an extra item of clothing under their shirts at the fancy boutiques where their mothers have charges. It's a no-crime crime to them. I mean, from the time they're born, their parents take every opportunity to tell them how they're constantly being overcharged for services, grossly overbilled for goods, because tradespeople love to milk the rich. But that was Hollister's business, not mine.

Unfortunately, once we were on the other side, all the wizard could produce were a couple of spades and a pair of shears. I stood for a long time in too much streetlight, the long shears weighing me down. I tried to remember what the air used to feel like around my old house, as if I was trying to remember my mother's scent without perfume. I looked for my sister standing with her knuckles gouged into her hips, telling my mother that if she was going to mope at home all day the least she could do was see that the backyard look presentable.

"A few rosebushes here, a line of daffodils there." Amanda circumscribed the landscape with her hands as she envisioned things. "A pond and a bridge would add considerable charm. But, for God's sake, the weeds have to be kept back and we need some of that icy-white lawn furniture. My God, something!" Amanda would say, setting her heels into my mother's difficult morning.

By that hour of the day my mother would have burned the breakfast or discovered she had left the milk out on the counter all night with the eggs and cheese, so there was nothing in the house to fix. Meanwhile, a box of Girl Scout cookies hid under the back steps where Mom sat. She waited for Amanda to go away so she could fill and level that place left by all the mistakes.

I even tried to conjure my father, his strange way of creeping around the wrong side of the house where no one ever passed except to check the gas meter. His pipe smoke drifting out ahead of him in the sign of a lazy morning, until he'd see my mother and sister squabbling over the large expanse of yard that would never be paid for. He'd stop and put his thumb over his pipe bowl. Just watch them for a while, making sure he wasn't detected. He'd even hunker down to observe them, smiling when my sister stomped off, watching the clear wrap from the Girl Scout cookie box drift over the lawn in the breeze.

I stopped the movie to see what had been altered since that time. As my eyes adjusted, I could make out new windows and window boxes; the back porch glassed in. The yard, however, remained virginal, as far as I could tell. The old shed was still erect, the flagstones in place. Hollister had a key-chain flashlight. I took him out to a far corner of the yard where the moss still grew in a strange configuration, right up into the crook of a willow—the shape formed like a woman's body or an old man's face, depending on where you stood.

He moved the narrow beam about. I told him this was the very spot where I'd intended to make it with my first guy; step off the face of the Earth when the spacecraft landed; fall into the soil when the bomb was dropped and. . . . I suddenly grew quiet, wondering why I was telling the break-and-enter man so much. I showed him where we had to dig.

Before he put his spade to that pretty lawn, he said: We moved too much.

As if to say the UFOs and bombs didn't know where to find him, I guess.

It took longer than I expected with our small tools, fighting that now-stable lawn. But eventually Hollister hit something. I gripped the flashlight in my teeth. As much as I was shaking, I worked with great care around his find. Eventually, we unearthed an old leather-bound book.

—I think there's another one, Hollister said.

Before long, he pulled two more volumes from the ground, their back covers coming free in the process, earthworms sliding over the raw pages. As if he were involved in a treasure hunt rather than an exhumation, Hollister wrestled several more tomes from the ground.

—Bring the flashlight, he said with an eager stride, moving into the center of the lawn. He began to dig anew.

I thought of stopping him, several times, but I held the light and watched. I don't know. For a while my heart pounded erratically, but then it seemed to disappear along with my ability to breathe. It was like seeing my father's face again, to see his books. Seeing him angry, I thought, angry that I'd forgotten something, a proper shovel, the color of his eyes, who knows. Like hearing him thunder about the way my memory had shut down over too many small objects on a tray.

I finally had to stop Hollister. He had made this crazy quilt of holes across the yard. Wherever he'd broken into the ground, there were more of my father's books—an entire library. The whole lawn was filled with his prized and very secretive collection, all his knowledge and wisdom, rotten through.

I told Hollister we had to go. We hadn't come to recover lost things, just to see the way they outsmart us. I returned all but one of the books. Hollister stuffed this into his shirt for me so we could climb back over the fence. He gave me a boost, knotting his fingers together in a tight hold. When I reached the top, an alarm went off, like a delayed reaction. Then, just as quick, it stopped. There wasn't time to think, but on the way back in the car we laughed and wondered why it hadn't gone off when we first went over. It was as if we'd discovered a sweet spot in the system.

Hollister decided it was probably designed to trap its victims *inside* the fence, creating easy work for the police.

In the end, since no one shouted or turned on lights, we decided the residents were probably on vacation, having fled the demands of a chronically faulty alarm system and the exhausting work of trying to secure their world. And by the time the neighbors were aroused, we were far away.

After several blocks, we came to a long stop. The red

light burned into the car and I took the book from Hollister. It was a slender volume of poetry. I wanted to imagine that my father had read even a line of poetry in his entire life, but the thought left me hungry. A headache started to move up from the base of my skull with a mocking throb. My father was, to be brief, a man of science. Science and strategy and confident reason. Calm torture. Not poetry.

—He loathed everything about me from the day I was born, I said.

Hollister was kind enough to listen.

—I remember running into his study in my first real shoes, chasing this rubber ball. But I fell and cut my forehead on his chair. He just squeezed that ball while he watched me. It would never have occurred to him to give the ball back or to see to my injury; he was much too intent on making me into one of his cases.

—I bet you were too reckless for him.

—Probably, I said, surprised that Hollister understood.

—I think my parents hoped I'd fall off a pier or get trampled under a polo pony. It would have been so much easier to raise a family tragedy than a flesh-and-blood child, he said.

—He was always trying to get me to reorganize my thoughts so I could win the game, I said.

—What game? Hollister asked, touching my thigh, resting all his energy there.

—He forced me to hear about it so often I don't think I ever understood it. My family was supposed to win at some kind of game. Well, probably not my mom. I think she was too lost for his purposes. Her game was lying on her mattress, hoping the day would be over. My mother was the one who stayed, but it took a long time to understand that she was his great failure . . . that each of us, in our own way, treated her like that. But Amanda and I . . . one of us anyway . . . we were supposed to win at something.

The sound of the car rushing over clean, dampened streets, the rhythm and comfort of lights flooding and draining from the car, the steady pressure of Hollister's hand, couldn't lull me. I suddenly realized I'd let my father leave without finding out enough about the game. I should have uprooted every book and found some way to take them with us, because each one was a clue into my father's mind.

I knew what would happen. The paint manufacturer would return home and call the police. The chief detective would have the whole yard dug up. He'd have to be pretty stupid or new to the department not to remember the address and that my father went missing while we lived in that house. An industrial Dumpster would be brought in for the books. The whole thing would be dug up in a day. The pathetic detective falling into book pits, book graves, twisting an ankle, cursing readers everywhere. The corpse eluding him.

The neighbors would recall the rumor of my father's library to him. An interest would flare up for a week or two. When nothing else could be unearthed, the owners would demand the detective either produce a body or return their yard to its original state. They would summon their attorneys. Finally the sod men would show up and a brief wildness in an uneventful neighborhood would be forced back into the earth by tamping machines. The gate locked, a new alarm system installed.

All I could do now was wait.

I was trying to explain this to Hollister—the way people have of being tribal even when they don't realize they're doing it. That there was no tribe where Amanda lived, as far as I could see—everyone staying in their apartments, bolts fastened, ordering out for groceries and meals, quickly getting in their cars, speeding off. I hadn't even seen the other people in Amanda's building—no one was trying to pry into anyone else's mailbox, not even to get an extra sample of free detergent.

Hollister and I were pretty high by then. He listened to my stories and breathed in the night air and tried to get his windshield completely washed. He fiddled with a million buttons on the dash to get rid of the bugs. I think Hollister was more good-natured than most. He had a remarkable sense of direction and calm, a handsome recall for street names and numbers.

Where I might have driven to Canada before I could find my mother's bed in the dark, Hollister had us right up to the door of the hospice in no time.

He killed the lights and asked: Now what?

It was dumb luck that the sidewalk was still warm, fireflies out, windows propped open. I ran across the lawn to a corner of the building and Hollister followed. We crouched down, so we were just under the lower lip of the first window. I popped my head up and peered inside. The bed in the first room looked empty. We continued down the row of rooms and sometimes I couldn't tell if anyone was inside, it was so dark, but I knew my mother relied on a soft light for going to sleep—a night-light she purchased for my sister or me once but had to steal away.

Finally I saw her glowing in the dark in a strange hospital bed. I left the rest to Hollister. He got the outer screen off without trouble and the window rode up easily. I guess they didn't worry too much about security. I mean, what do you take from someone who's dying?

Hollister boosted me inside and whispered that he'd wait in the car, that I should take all the time I wanted. I had this funny inclination; I mean I wanted to introduce him to my mother. But instead I leaned out to him and kissed his face, said I wouldn't be long.

I expected a network of tubes and cords to be connected to my mother, but there was only one tube that I could see, from a drip bottle to her chest, I imagined, into her heart. I figured that was the morphine. Or it should have been if it wasn't. She was thinner than the last time I saw her. Actually, visibly thinner. Her hair was matted into the pillow making her look like something wild, the way I thought my mother probably looked before she was my mother.

I've never figured why she and my father thought they had the right to keep so much from us. They never would tell me, or my sister as far as I knew, the simplest things, like how they'd met. As if some unpleasant beginning was too potent a thing to hold in our hands and study, even for a second. Maybe they worried that it was something we'd identify in our own lives later on, like objects placed on a tray. I think Amanda had been right, in a roundabout way. Not that my mother was Dad's patient as she insisted, because I don't think Mom was always so troubled. I think that came after her marriage began.

No, my belief was that she was the wife of one of his patients. Instead of our father being attracted to something injured, fundamentally damaged, as Amanda would have me think, I decided he slowly seduced the young, buxom wife of a schizophrenic man, say. In time, he had the man institutionalized (there probably wasn't much more he could do for him in those days). Then my father proceeded to take that patient's wife right on his office couch with his bizarre authority, certainly with complete disregard for my mother's future or his own place in society, since he seemed so determined not to have one.

For some odd reason, that's what I wanted to know more than anything that night: how my parents met. Not about my father's disappearance or some island in the Bahamas or the books in the yard or if my father was the one to push my mother steadily into the folds of her bedroom—where her eyes were open and food boxes lay empty around her like violent dreams.

I soaked a washcloth in warm water to wake my mother. There are few places more depressing than the bathroom of a medical facility. Always some kind of pads or syringes or metal bowls stacked up, ready to torture the patient. The room itself wasn't much better. There was one stiff chair for a visitor and another bed that was empty and stripped of linens. Over the two beds, terrible sea art in uncomfortable frames; it was a kindness that my mother couldn't see those images from where she lay.

I ran the washcloth over her face as gently as I could. She woke up when her face cooled—she used to wake us that way sometimes—and she smiled at me as if I had been there all night, as if I lived in the nursing facility with her.

—Are you all right? I said.

She wanted to answer that she was fine, I could tell by her expression, but she began to cough a thick, chesty cough. I was afraid someone was going to burst through the door, but she finally stopped. Then she just smiled again, as if this was all her greatest effort could produce. I wanted to climb into bed with her, to curl around her soft body, but the bed was much too small; it was barely big enough to contain my mother. I imagined the pain she had in turning to her other side or onto her back. They probably made her do this several times a day because they can never leave you alone.

She pointed to a glass of water and I put the straw to her mouth. I watched the weak sips she took and how some dribbled back out. She began to cough again and coughed for a long time.

I heard someone in the hall and slid under the bed. There was a crack of light as a nurse opened the door, just to check, I guess. Maybe my mother had always been my one real ally, because I felt instinctively that she made herself stop coughing somehow and closed her eyes, pretending to sleep, so the woman would disappear, which she did.

When I pulled myself back up and looked at my mother's face, I finally realized something about her death. It would be very soon and very unreal and very horrible. She would take the worst of the family secrets with her, as if they were part of her body now—all that food she never really wanted to eat. And she would take my comfort.

I touched her face. I told her Amanda and I were getting along much better. I said she was helping me pick out colleges and I was getting excited about finishing high school. I told her I loved the new school and had made lots of friends; a few of them had been over to the apartment. After that, I'm not sure what I said. I went on for quite a while and I could tell how pleased she was. That's one thing Amanda and I always knew about our mother, that she just wanted to hear the pleasant things, the things lighter than thought.

I wasn't going to make her talk, but that's the way it was with us. I mean maybe the sickness was holding her tongue—maybe she felt certain the smallest word would rouse her lungs again and remind her that she was leaving me—but it was her way, to want me to sit on the edge of her bed or lie down beside her, and let me talk and never require that she say a word. I think it was the only way she had of teaching me to be kind.

I watched as she shut her eyes and drifted for a long time; I was grateful that there wasn't a clock to look at. There was part of me that wasn't really sure if she'd ever been awake, much as I felt certain she was asleep now. I kissed her on the lips and promised to come back in a couple of days, and told her not to worry about anything. Then I worked at getting the bad sea art off the walls. Once I had it down, I lowered each frame outside the window before I climbed out and left with them under one arm.

Hollister was leaning against his car, watching, eager for me.

—How is she? he asked. He put the prints in his trunk without asking me why I had them, then he opened the door for me and I got in his car and turned toward my window right away so he couldn't see how shaken I was.

—She wasn't too bad, I said.

He fired up the car.

—Did you get to talk?

—We talked so much I thought we couldn't talk anymore, and we laughed so hard we almost got caught, I said.

—I know it's a hospice but is there a chance . . . ?

—Maybe.

Hollister drove us down to the beach and got out a couple of blankets from the trunk and we slept on the sand. Sometimes I think we made love that night and sometimes I think I cried all night instead of sleeping. But maybe it was all of that, crying and sleeping and thrashing around with Hollister just under the sound of the surf. If I'd been any less tired I might have worried that the water would lap up to our blankets in the middle of the night and take us off.

My father's life was too invested in plans, even if they were based on miserable notions, and my mother was about the business of unraveling plans, which was probably her saving grace. My sister's success was built on what she referred to as "flexible plans"—which meant she could be bought and sold.

I liked to think I just didn't have any plans so there was nothing to come undone. But I knew what my sister deserved, after seeing my mother that night, in such a place, with the bad sea art—which Hollister and I launched onto the Outer Drive. There wasn't enough oxygen in the entire city to keep her lungs quiet, and the rest I couldn't name because there wasn't anything else to name in her room. Just the gradual loss of personality Amanda must have wished for my mother in the end.

Even without a plan of my own, I understood the prize to come. It would be that moment that would fly out of all the moments that preceded it, when I'd look at poor Amanda and tell her about my high treason with Nathaniel.

Hollister insisted we get breakfast. I thought I wasn't hungry, but I ate everything the waitress brought out of the kitchen.

He was a funny sort, Hollister. We went over to a restaurant called Googles—two big, lunatic eyes in the double *O*s of the sign enticing us to come on in. We managed to get seats at the counter before the lunch crush.

Googles was a restaurant for the androgynous night prowlers who stopped in for long coffees and meringue pies after the transvestite bars closed. I remember how my sister once warned me never to go into a "place like that," as we passed by in her car, as if all that masquerade and ambivalence could harm me. But Sharon had taken me there a couple of times—and I had watched her flirt with people of questionable origin in a comfortable way. That was the thing I most admired about Sharon, the way she traveled in different worlds, even if she relied on doormen to open most of the doors for her.

Anyway, Googles was for families in the daytime, and a great number of them would come from the newly opened van Gogh exhibit that afternoon, with words about art and cruelty, squinting at the day, trying to adjust their visuals back to the greylands like returning to the wrong side of the mirror.

I forget now if I ordered three breakfasts or four. But I'm certain I had a malted, and that cottage fries came with everything, and I had to send the waitress after a second bottle of ketchup. I ate the way my mother often ate before her illness—but there wasn't much time for self-loathing when we parted company with Googles. I felt so happy to be returned to my body; it really was like falling straight from the mind into the stomach. The few thoughts I could muster were sluggish, disjointed, even pleasant. I wondered if it was that way with my mother when she ate to bring the house down.

It was a still, quiet Saturday by the time we finished. I knew Hollister wanted to sneak back into my sister's apartment and crash on the spare bed in the guest room with me. But I needed some time to think. So I made him drive off and I took the El. I didn't care if it was the A train or the B train or some new letter just invented. I just got on the first car that opened in front of me, leaned my head against a window and felt the air come up from the bottom of the city. It rushed against my face and I knew I couldn't breathe without that great force of oxygen pounding me, taking me past the cemetery and a thousand pictures spray-painted along its endless concrete wall.

ELEVEN

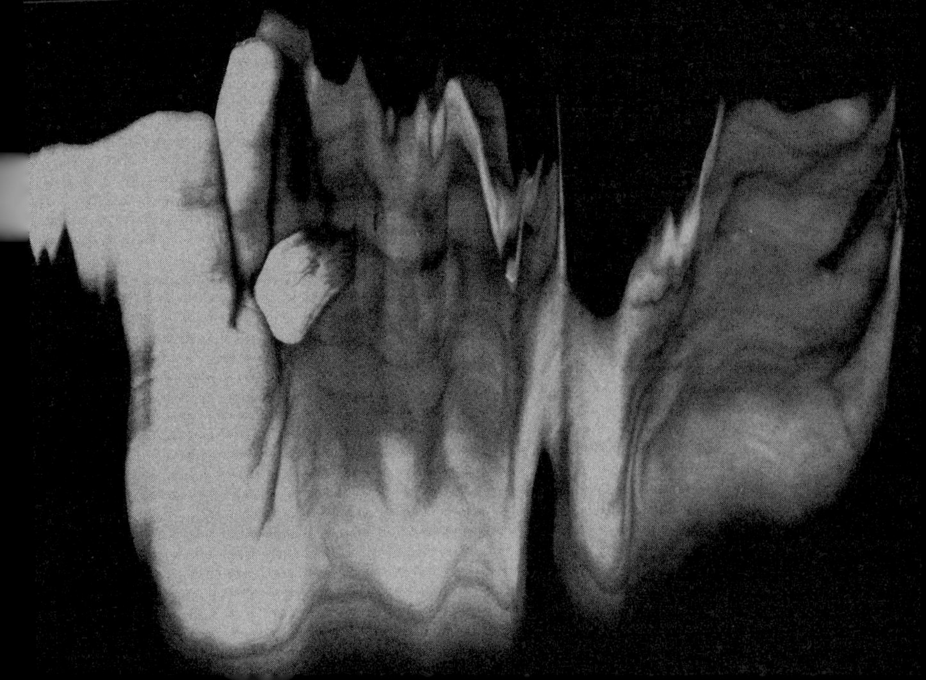

WHAT DID MY FATHER SAY? LIFE IS AN INCOMPLETE DREAM?

There were those periods when he was curious about my dreams. I was supposed to go into them in detail, as I squirmed in one of his office chairs. I tried to make enticing reports. But after a while he showed little interest in the bizarre plots and fine details. All he really wanted to know was whether or not I had been "aware" when I dreamed. There were things I could control and manipulate within my dreams or at least be cognizant of, he said. I could look at my feet or hands, or direct the car I was rid-ing in to go in a different direction. I could even remind myself I was having a dream. When I failed at this, he told me I needed to find a place to sleep, other than my bedroom.

But he left us right after that.

As soon as we moved to Wharton Manor I looked for the right place. I tried the ballroom but it was so big my thoughts drifted up to the ceiling and caught there; and I always associated my mother with that room. Amanda staked out the little house in the garden, which meant the whole garden was hers. I roamed the maids' quarters—but the spare rooms were dreamless places, and then Mr. Graf moved in eventually.

In my waking hours, I never considered that there might be something to stand away from and observe, to manipulate. My mother's grief was always too tactile. The smell of her bedding as I lay down to comfort her in the shadows, the sound of my sister slamming doors from one end of the house to the other and back again, the miserable schools—the things they wrote on your locker about your family.

I began to keep a diary. I recorded both dreams and daydreams, hoping my father wouldn't notice the difference. I thought that with something in hand I could show him a sense of accomplishment when he returned.

Looking back, after Mr. Graf moved in, most of my daydreams were about him. I know I spent a lot of time investigating and trying to add up clues. If I saw something poking out of the trash that I knew couldn't possibly belong to my mother or sister, I made careful observations, noting them in my diary. If I heard a particular noise coming from the back of the house, I'd go up to the second floor and press my ear or a drinking glass against the adjoining door. That would get noted along with the date and hour.

As time went on, I grew bolder and liked to slip into his side of the manor, hiding in a dark turn in the hall. I hoped he'd get on the phone so I could hear his voice, but he never did. He stayed in that one room and kept the door shut, if he was there at all. I took out several books from the school library on criminology and spying techniques. But I never had enough money to purchase a listening device, and when I tried to capture his fingerprints, I dropped a full box of my mother's favorite dusting powder—which made me feel particularly bad because I knew I couldn't replace it.

Meantime, my mother and sister kept up their secret and very separate rendezvous with Mr. Graf. An average of once a week Amanda would let herself in through the adjoining doors when she knew our mother was out and thought I had gone to bed or was so occupied I wouldn't care where she was. With the same frequency my mother would sneak around to his outside door, when she was certain my sister was off somewhere. I think she assumed I was too young to be interested in what she did with whom.

During this entire time, I thought both my sister and mother were having hypnosis sessions with Mr. Graf. I noticed the incremental but very real changes in both of them. My sister was withdrawing in a way I had never seen before. Her bitterness toward my mother was so sharp it was as if she were sliding it back and forth over a grindstone all day. To the same degree, my mother blossomed. Though she had always hated to iron so much as a fancy handkerchief, now she wouldn't leave the house without a perfectly pressed outfit. The warm smell of perfume around her wrists and neck, a slight drop down her bosom. She began to have heels mended on shoes she had been content to wear to the nails and glue before. And the slow introduction of the little tunes she hummed in the halls and kitchen suddenly reminded me that this was something she used to do all the time when I was small.

If this was Mr. Graf's doing, which I was sure it was, I certainly began to wonder after his purpose. I worried about what life would be like for my mother when Mr. Graf suddenly moved from our back rooms. Amanda must have been one of his failed experiments.

I wouldn't have had any problem about marching right up to either of Mr. Graf's doors and introducing myself, but I felt certain Amanda would get word of it. Maybe I dreaded all the hours and days of trying to apologize to her, so she'd settle down again. I tried to think of ways to blackmail her into telling me what this Mr. Graf was up to, but she was impossible to blackmail; she kept her tracks covered.

So, it was a desperate August day when I came home from school with the decision to smoke him out. I planned to start a pan of bacon drippings smoking on the stove, so I could scream FIRE at the top of my lungs.

I had just scooped the fat into the pan, the gas flame up to its white peak, when I saw the top of my mother's head as she darted through the bushes around the side of the kitchen. She was all dressed up as if she'd just come from work, with a look that told me she'd been in the maids' quarters.

I heard her key in the front door and a much too cheery: Hello!

I stepped out of the living room and cornered her in the foyer.

—You look nice, I said.

—Why thank you, dear. How was your day?

We were not the kind of family to ask such a question, so I didn't say anything as I threw my arms around her neck. She was confused, embarrassed really, and probably didn't understand that I wanted to sniff her hair.

—You're wearing perfume again, I said, releasing her.

—Oh, I guess so. I must have put it on this morning.

—Really? It's so strong. It's almost like cologne, I said.

I watched my mother turn a difficult color and look around, as if she'd forgotten a package in the car.

—I think I'll lie down for a little while before I start supper.

—I really need some help with my homework. Just twenty minutes. Please.

—Well . . . alright, she said, letting me direct her toward the kitchen. I turned to see her smooth down her dress, as if it might be caught up in the back.

—It's almost like cigar smoke or something, I said.

—What is? she smiled, softening to the idea of helping me with my homework, of being needed, functioning as a family—all the things she wanted but could never seem to fulfill.

—Your cologne, I mean, perfume. It makes me think of cigars, I said.

—God almighty! my mother yelled and flew through the kitchen door. A great pipe of black smoke curled against the ceiling and spread out in an umbrella. I was about to throw water on the pan but my mother stopped me. She took over, using an entire box of baking soda. She hoisted windows that were often stuck and fanned the smoke with a section of newspaper.

—What on earth were you trying to do, Molly? my mother said.

—It's . . . my science project. I guess I don't really understand what I'm supposed to do, I said.

—Maybe you could ask your teacher to explain it a little better before you try it again.

My mother sat down at the table and watched the tails of black smoke float through the room.

—You're right, I said, sitting down across from her. I put my feet up on the chair in between.

—You want some tea? I promise not to set it on fire, I assured her.

—I'll do it, Molly.

She made each of us a cup of tea, hers with extra sugar, mine so plain she always wondered at my taste. Then she put her feet up on the other chair and we both blew at our cups. I thought about our kitchen, how it probably knew more disasters than anything else, more ruined dinners and sour times.

—Does he hypnotize you? I said.

—Does what? Does who hypnotize me? she said, her

mouth doing something coy and frightening around the worn lipstick.

—Mr. Graf, I said.

—Oh. Mr. Graf, she said.

—You don't have to pretend. I see you go over there all the time.

—Does Amanda . . . do you think she's aware . . . ? my mother started to say.

—I don't know. Does Mr. Graf hypnotize you?

—You don't have to worry about Mr. Graf, Molly. He's not . . . he's not . . . permanent. He's just someone to spend a little time with. You'll understand when you get older, she said.

—But you're not answering me. Does he put you under?

—Mr. Graf doesn't really practice hypnosis anymore, my mother explained.

—But he used to. That's what he was, right? A hypnotist?

—I try not to pry too much, Molly, she said, as if this would finish the discussion.

—So why do you spend time with him?

—Maybe I shouldn't. I don't want it to upset you, sweetheart.

—It isn't upsetting me. I've been reading books on hypnosis all year and I need to interview him for a very important school paper, I said.

—He'd never do that.

—But the paper counts for seventy percent of my grade, I pleaded.

—I'm sorry, Molly. Maybe we can come up with someone else for you to interview.

—I know he hypnotizes you, I said.

—He doesn't, dear.

—You keep a weekly appointment with him.

—Maybe we should drop it, Molly. I really should get a little rest in before I start dinner.

—No, you don't need a little rest. You need to tell me what's going on. Amanda and you each going over there. I could set all the clocks in the house by your visits.

—Amanda does that?

—It's science fiction. Neither of you wants the other to know, and I know he's doing something to you—some kind of experiment. So I'm just going to go over there and find out for myself.

I stood up and pushed the chair away.

That's when we heard Amanda come home and throw her things down on the hall table.

Without anyone saying hello, we watched her come into the kitchen and over to the freezer where she pushed the icy objects around looking for a quick dinner, a Popsicle, anything.

I looked at my mother's eyes and the fragile veins broken through on her cheeks. She was terrified that I was going to tell my sister. But I was thinking how we all owned a secret now. A secret around Mr. Graf. That we made this stranger the center of something—we gave him an importance beyond each other.

So I decided to wait a little longer to confront him, and

left my mother and my sister in the kitchen with their prisoners' silence.

There's a reason they call it the Loop. Because you can get on one of those elevated trains and keep looping back on yourself until you finally feel like you're getting somewhere. As soon as my head began to clear I knew I had to find Nathaniel and get a few things straight with him about my sister before he destroyed his life and "our chance at happiness" as the movie line goes.

I stopped in a drugstore downtown and used the pay phone. I couldn't reach him at his house so I called the number he didn't want me to use—the one at his office. I was afraid he was going to blow up or something but he told me to stay where I was; he'd be over in a taxi.

I'm still convinced that people really can change, in a second flat. I've watched it happen to every single member of my family. My father fueled by his corruption of us—and then gone, vanished. My mother living in new stockings and last hopes—then chemically altered, her body suddenly eating itself from the inside out. Even Amanda, running out of her game, altering the course of her life with the sudden impulse to marry. I've learned to watch for that moment, trying to catch it midair. As if there's a volatile, molten part to us that you can register in the eye as it goes off. I thought I saw it in Nathaniel that day. He was suddenly buoyant, playful, not to be dissuaded from the thing that resembled a cause to him. I thought I could recognize the course of change in him, or I let myself believe I could.

Of all crazy things, he wanted to take me shopping. I told him I didn't need any clothes, but the more I said it the more I felt like I was talking with Amanda. I didn't care where we went as long as we could talk to the point of obsession; that's all that mattered. But he took me to Saks. Dreaded Saks Fifth Avenue. Amanda's store.

We took an elevator that was hidden away in a back corner of the store. He guided me to this sanctum sanctorum on the second floor, an intimate showroom with its own dressing room for preferred customers. I dropped into a slouchy chair and waited for the next act. A severe-looking woman joined us—one of Saks's fashion guards. Nathaniel moved in close to her bones—there wasn't much else to her—and whispered long and hard in her ear as if he was revealing something about sex that she'd never even considered.

He pulled me out of the chair.

—Now you follow her, he said.

—I'm tired of clothes, I said, hoping that was what any self-respecting model would say. But I followed her.

I came out of the dressing room wearing an evening gown. It was white like a holdover from a wedding and would have made anyone think of Audrey Hepburn if I were that thin, my neck that swanlike. Nathaniel paced and smoked. He still hadn't removed his sunglasses. He laughed to himself when he saw me. The woman pushed my shoulders back to make me taller.

—Let's see the next one, he told her.

I liked the next outfit though I wasn't sure why. It was the last thing in the world I'd ever wear in public. There was something very Japanese about it, and tight-fitting. Maybe it was the feel of the silk. Strictly cocktail-party stuff. Once again he smiled to himself and waved me back to the dressing room.

There were eight outfits in all. Each one a different personality. A new identity. Old money. New money. Housewife, schoolgirl, corporate wife. One was strictly lingerie. That got no response at all, which really confused me. When I was in career-girl clothes—a tidy suit that could go day or evening, the woman said—I tried to stop the show. I went over and sat in his lap. He gave me a peck on the cheek and sent me off to change again.

The last was a dress, ankle-length with crisscross straps in the back, a full skirt, with big, bright colors. There was so much spring in it, I felt as if the carpet of our private dressing rooms had turned to grass, that the ceiling fixtures were rays of sun hitting me. I stood in front of the vault of mirrors, hoping I'd finally pleased him. But I wasn't any good to Nathaniel that way. I was more naked than I'd been in that syrupy lingerie. I couldn't help but cry because I didn't know enough about him yet, enough details—I was afraid I'd never figure out a way to memorize Nathaniel.

—I just . . . want to talk, I said, the tears dropping onto the new fabric.

Either he sent the woman away or she left on her own accord. Maybe he handed her some money or whispered to her that someone in my family was dying. Maybe he told her he'd take all the outfits but just give us a few minutes. In any case, he took me from the seating area to the inner dressing room, clothes everywhere. He pushed me up against the mirror and began to kiss me. I opened my eyes and saw a million copies of us in the glass, none of them real. He cut into the spring, into the madness, and I began to babble questions, fragments of questions.

—Do you think the Earth . . . ? By fire? Will it go by fire? Are you really . . . ? I'm not sure that I can. . . .

He moved me down into the chair and pulled my legs apart. No one would ever love me like that again. His mouth swallowed thought after thought.

When he penetrated me, he drew the skirt of my dress over my face, over my mouth. I thought of Amanda's mouth moving through the gauze of her lifted nightgown to say: spider bites.

Everything was so quick and confused with Nathaniel. He said: There's no way this could ever work, you know.

But it was killing him to say it; I could see that. It was the way his eyes looked. Everything inside of him wanted to make it work. He helped me back into my clothes, as if he had nothing else in the world to do but undress and dress me and worry that things might not work out.

—Are you hungry? he said.

—I have no idea.

—You make a lousy model, he said, smiling. It was obvious that he enjoyed my fragile attempts at deceit.

He looked at his watch.

—Jesus. Where can I drop you? he said.

Maybe there really wasn't anywhere to go but Sharon's.

I stayed in her shower so long a nuclear warhead could have fried Sharon into a noonday shadow outside, and I wouldn't have noticed. Then I put on her guest bathrobe, the steam rising from my hair. Sharon's maid tiptoed into the room with two ice-cold Cokes. We watched her in deadly silence.

—You look fagged, Sharon said after she'd gone.

—I haven't been sleeping well, I said, belting back the Coke.

Sharon gave me that look, like I was just cellophane on the outside, mere Saran Wrap. When she saw me drain my glass, she picked up her phone and told the maid we were dying for Coke in there—*dying.* And Sharon's will be done, because her life was a place in time that refused to run out of anything.

The maid thing was so bad that before my thirst could be slaked I had to stop drinking so this middle-aged woman would stop tapping on the door with her felt-tip fingers, her gentle pussy feet crossing the carpet to refill my glass. After a while it was like having a cut and thinking someone else could bleed for you.

I was lying down on Sharon's guest bed, my arms crucified, legs splayed into the downy bedding, when Sharon's voice woke me.

—You aren't going to sleep, are you?

—Not really. I sat up and reached for one of the cigarettes. Sharon looked at the ceiling, blowing smoke rings like broken skulls into the air. I watched the long shadows from the park travel across her ceiling.

—What the hell are you doing to poor Hollister? Sharon said at last. She began to choke on too much cigarette and unspoken news.

—What am I doing to him?

She fanned the fingers of one hand and cracked them against her thigh.

—I didn't think you even knew the guy.

—I don't, I said.

—Well, you can tell that to his monkey. He called me up at seven this morning. Seven A.M. on a Saturday morning! He's lost it completely, she said, cracking her other hand on her opposite thigh.

I didn't know what to say, which irritated her to no end.

—Will you stop it and tell me what happened? Sharon said.

—You're saying he's angry with me about something?

—Jesus Christ. No, he's not angry with you about something. He's crazy about you. What did you do to him? she said.

—Other than the usual? I grinned, still not understanding.

—If you don't . . . , Sharon said. She threw a pillow at me and hit the ashtray square on.

I looked at the ash sprinkled over her guest robe.

—We just . . . I don't know. It seems like a long time ago, to tell you the truth, I said.

—A long time ago?! Yesterday is a long time ago? Sharon said.

—Look, we just spent some time together. It wasn't anything, I said, starting to brush the ash off.

—Leave it. Bridget will clean up later. You better hope his folks don't find out, she sniffed.

—Thanks a lot.

I stubbed out my cigarette in the empty ashtray so she could hear each little crush of tobacco and paper.

—I don't mean . . . you're so sensitive, Molly. I told you about them.

—He doesn't mean a thing in the world, I said, standing up and watching ash fall to the ground. Thinking about volcanoes. Thinking about Amanda.

—Then why bother the poor boy?

—What did he say exactly?

I began to look around for my clothes.

—It was a regular CIA investigation. He wanted to know everything. If you were seeing someone and . . .

—What did you tell him?

—I said you were a simple, sweet girl who . . .

—Bullshit.

—OK, I said there might be someone but I wasn't sure. I also said I didn't know a great deal about your family, but I knew your mother was pretty ill and that you were living with your sister for the time being. Is that *alright*?

—I guess that's alright, I said.

—Hollister's just the wrong guy to pick on. I don't mean pick on. But shit, Molly. If he doesn't mean anything, why get him all worked up? Hollister gets hurt easily, you know. And you have to understand the families. I mean, if his mother finds out, she's going to be calling my mother, and somehow I'm going to be responsible for everything.

—I don't mean he doesn't mean a thing exactly, I said, beginning to comb out my wet hair, hoping the little droplets of water would fly in her direction.

—But you just said that. You just said he doesn't mean a thing in the world to you.

—I . . . I just spent a little time with him. And I wouldn't have if I'd known everyone was going to find out so fast and jump on me, I said.

—Everyone hasn't found out. I'm just trying to keep it that way, Sharon said.

—I'd swear I'm talking to your mother, I said.

Absolute silence, fine drops of water. Then Sharon gave it away with a single look.

—So how . . . was he? she said.

—Better, I said.

—Meaning? she said.

—Than I expected. Tender, I guess.

She nodded.

—Look . . . Hollister and I have been going to school together since kindergarten. And his folks and my folks have been socializing since forever.

—And you're in love with him but you forgot to tell me, I said.

—God, no. It's just . . . you know, you get curious. I'm glad to hear he's tender. It fits, she said.

But it was obvious now. Sharon was in love with Hollister, even if it was a flighty, jealous love; something she'd never pursue if left to her own doing.

—Look, I better go. I'm sure my sister's looking for me, I said.

—Call her from here, Sharon insisted in a listless way.

—No, I really should go back to the apartment and get some fresh clothes and . . .

—Clothes? God, help yourself. I get so sick of my clothes.

I didn't want to, but I knew I'd only make matters worse if I rejected her by turning down her offer. So I dressed while Sharon looked at me, studied me. I held my stomach in and got her jeans zipped with some effort. I looked for an old T-shirt, but Sharon didn't have old T-shirts. I had to settle for something ironed; I refused to borrow her socks even though she tried to give me several pairs, the way she foisted her rubbers on me. I ran a lipstick over my lips and was about to leave when she sprang it on me.

—Look, Molly. I'm sorry if I hurt your feelings. It's just the timing.

I rummaged in my purse for the last transfer I'd purchased to see if it was still good.

—The story in the paper, she said.

—In the paper, I said absently.

—You saw it, didn't you? she said.

Sharon reached under the dust ruffle of her bed and pulled out the morning edition of the *Sun Times.* Her family took all the editions, her mother a chronic browser of the society pages, her father forever anxious over stocks. Sharon handed me a folded section of paper with a very old picture of my father. And there was also a picture of a backhoe digging into my old yard, and a hound-dog detective holding up a stack of worm-eaten books with some pride.

I could feel the earth in the pit of my stomach.

—You know there was a Swedish man who used to eat books. I mean entire libraries. He claimed that his stomach could read every word that way and that he had total recall. They tested the man. No one could stump him, Sharon said, throwing herself back on the bed.

I snapped my purse shut and looked at Sharon as she reclined into the comfort of the life she would always fall back on.

—You're going to have a tough time showing your face at school on Monday, Molly. I guess I could go with you if you want.

Whatever else Sharon said was sucked up by her thick carpet and her heavy drapes, the hush of her maids' shoes and the inside of her parents' lives. I took the article with me and tried to read it in the elevator, but the newsprint blurred and the picture washed out, the ink ran off the edges of the paper. Still, I knew what it said, what the evening news would say.

There was a rehash of my father's disappearance. They were considering reopening the case, but it was too soon to tell. They'd have to see what they dug up. Ha, ha. Someone would make that pun without fail. It was a situation ripe for puns, and the evening news, Amanda kept telling me, had become a struggle for a better pun, a higher rating. I threw the newspaper in the trash when I got outside.

I began to feel like one of those people forced to leave her country for political reasons.

There was a Laundromat, not far from Amanda's apartment, where I spent the rest of the day. I remember how shocked Amanda acted when she heard about the murder there the month before, as if she really thought she could pick an area of the city immune to life and death. Seems a man tried to steal an old woman's purse but she refused to give it up, so he killed her. All she had was change for the washers and dryers. No hairbrush or face powder or worn tickets to foreign lotteries. She just made it valuable by holding onto it so hard.

While I was sitting there, I tried to figure out why there was an entire dryer filled with nothing but children's pajamas, the kind with the feet sewn in. All of them running around the hot glass of the dryer door; no one very interested in retrieving them. Someone must have chunked a day's supply of quarters into the machine or maybe it was broken, because it refused to stop.

I couldn't imagine in all the world why anyone had so many children. And I certainly couldn't imagine why anyone ever had Amanda and me.

TWELVE

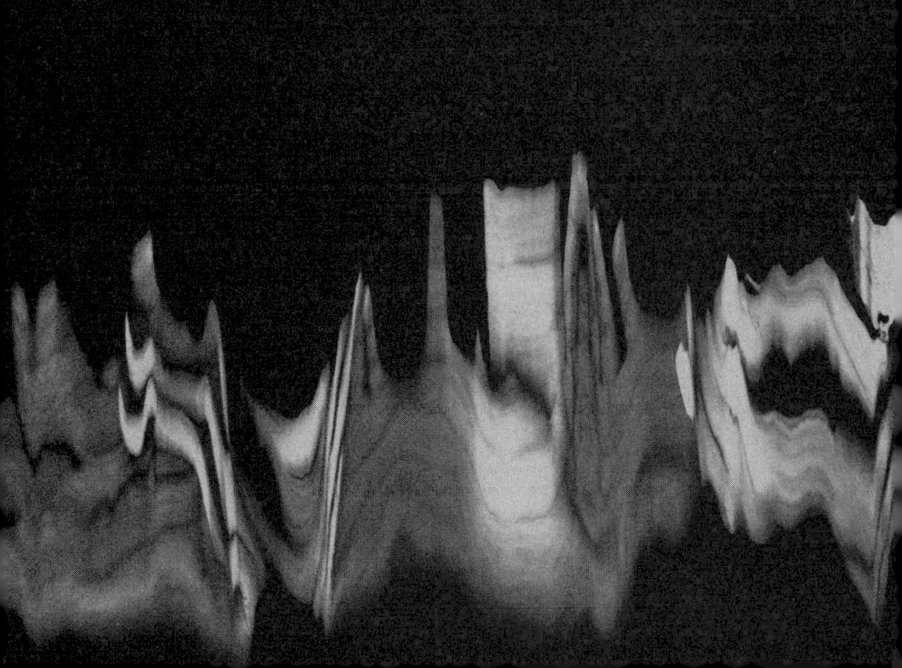

WHEN THE LAUNDROMAT STOPPED SPINNING FOR THE night, I went back to Amanda's. She was out but her craziness was there, waiting for me. The lipstick on the hall mirror was bright as fake blood. It read: WHAT THE FUCK ARE YOU DOING, MOLLY?!

I considered this for a long time.

I went into the bathroom and read: I HATE YOUR FUCKING GUTS!

That was my sister; hold nothing in reserve.

The mirror in the powder room read: DON'T TALK TO ANYONE ABOUT FATHER!

The large, antique mirror in the hall said: LISTEN TO THE MACHINE!

And the full-length mirror inside her bedroom closet read: CONSIDER YOURSELF ORPHANED; I DO!

I knew it pained my sister to leave such notes. Wherever she was, she was frantic because she wasn't able to have this episode in front of me. I was sure she was over at Nathaniel's, giving him the brunt of her temper.

I kept thinking that maybe Amanda would finally realize he wasn't going to be any better at patching her together than he was at bailing her out. I could almost hear her shoes storming away from his apartment. If it hadn't happened already, I knew it was imminent. I was prepared, in that event, to show up at Nathaniel's door in one of my sister's negligees under one of her raincoats, holding that old suitcase of my father's.

I was starting to pack, weeding out the dirty clothes from the dirtier ones, deciding which things of Amanda's I needed more than she did, when I remembered the message machine.

The first message was from the flack who wrote the article on our father. Did Amanda know about the books in the yard? Did she know where her father was? He pitched the simple idea of having her story told the way it should be told.

This was followed by a call from the housekeeper, to see if she could switch days.

Then this golden call: Hey, this is Dave. Um. I was sent

out from the pest-control agency the other day. Look, I don't like doing this over the phone but this would be a particularly bad time to get a call back at the office and I live with my girlfriend. . . . Um. I've been trying to call you. I think I've called twenty times already. So if I get you in hot water, I'm really sorry. But if I didn't call you'd be even more pissed. Um. Look, if you can just think of this like controlling an invading insect population—that there's a tried-and-true compound to destroy it. And that penicillin has an organic base. Um. I think you probably have the clap. I don't really know if I gave it to you or the other way around, so maybe it doesn't matter. God, I hate message machines. Look, I've got to go. I hope the spiders aren't bothering you. Sorry there wasn't time to do the spraying the day I came out. I've told my boss there was a mix-up on the address. So just call up to reschedule and my partner will come out—no questions asked. Okay? He doesn't know about this other stuff. Okay? Well . . . see you.

That was the last message on the machine and probably the real reason for Amanda's rage—the spiders. I don't think she knew how our father's books had surfaced—even if she suspected me. It would have been much worse if she knew it all. She would have been Lizzie Borden driving through the city in search of her only sibling. No, it was the spiders, the latest pestilence moving through her life in biblical proportions. She couldn't take being let down, even by me.

Sometimes, when the game gets too complicated, you have to find the smallest thing in the world to solve. My father used to say that about getting stuck in a chess game or a crossword puzzle. The best thing, he said, is to divert yourself—to fix something else, something entirely unrelated. He liked to repair light switches, even the ones that seemed to be in perfect working order. Or find a single screw in a hinge that could afford a modest amount of tightening.

I got all of Amanda's art books—well, Mom's art books really—and spread them out on my sister's living-room floor. Gauguin was Mother's favorite and the prints were very old and particularly fine. She was crazy for the Impressionists and Post-Impressionists and really had a handsome collection of art books.

I should say I was certain those books were never art but simply commerce for Amanda. She'd sell them at some point to the highest bidder and pride herself on holding onto them until the market was just right. For my mother and me they were like small rooms to hide in.

My mother was an artist once. It's hard to say what happened. Sometimes I think my father drove the painting out of her. He was, for all his standoffish ways, the hours spent over his books locked in his study, a man who required a great deal—always sending my mother on errands, forcing her into the world he vehemently shunned. And then, after he left, she had to work. . . . I had convinced myself that the death of her art was like the loss of a baby. Something she never wanted to talk about, couldn't get over.

I cut pictures out of all the books, the prints she liked the best. I wanted to frame them, but I didn't have that kind of time. Putting them up with masking tape would have to do. It would be just fine with Gauguin, I reasoned.

He would understand my frenetic need to change my mother's barren walls.

When I was done, I rolled the prints up, put rubber bands around them and eased them into my backpack. I put the books back on the shelves and cleaned up the scraps of paper. After I left Amanda's apartment, I, too, felt a kind of emptiness, as if someone had cut pictures out of me. I was the backyard from which the books had been pulled. All the hiding places used up.

I had to find someplace to spend the night and I remembered the all-night theater Sharon had pointed out in our travels. She said that they mostly played French movies with subtitles. Some of the movies were erotic, and some were edgy films about love blowing up, most of them pornographic. The actors smoked cigarettes like mad and fucked each other in black and white. She warned me that there was often some couple who did it in the back of the theater, the light bouncing off the screen, exposing them periodically.

That's where I went, the all-night theater.

I flashed one of Amanda's expired IDs, which the guy at the door didn't even check, and walked in in the middle of a movie. I wasn't really up for reading subtitles, so I just settled in with plenty to eat. I had to marvel at the stock of films they had and the variety of snacks. I put an entire meal together in that little theater, while the black-and-white light took me. The soothing French words of the actors charmed until I arrived in another state.

But that movie ended abruptly and another one started. The next film was made in the Forties—a game of strip poker, two women with strange hairdos, bathed in the glow of stark sex. Two men who kept licking their chops right into the lens. The editing and burned film left half of it to the imagination and when they started screwing the film sped up. I thought about how we're all animals, just insects moving in and out of a quick life. I felt something turning cold inside—and I thought if I didn't do something fast, it might just freeze over. I realized I couldn't stop the past. Or the slow bleed I was doing over Nathaniel.

It's hard to explain what it was about Nathaniel. It wasn't the sex, really. It wasn't about him being my sister's boyfriend—she had so many, and they all came and went without altering her personality in the least. It never was about mundane things. I knew he'd teach me something about music; I'd take him to art shows. We'd order out night after night because neither of us would cook. We'd find ways to tempt each other, frighten each other to inch closer to railings, train tracks, elevator shafts. But it wasn't that. It was more like knowing how things were going to be with him, without the slightest doubt. I mean, if Amanda had prophetic dreams—which I still question to this day—I thought I had a way of seeing the future by looking into Nathaniel's face, even from a long way off. I knew, in time, Nathaniel and I would talk without end, without the hope of ever finding an end or a need for one. I'd never find anyone else to talk with the way I could talk with Nathaniel; that's what I held onto when everything else began to disappear.

I went out to the lobby and called him. There wasn't an answer.

I called Sharon but she hung up on me.

I went back inside and lost myself in that movie house until it became a bright, glaring Sunday outside and I was convinced I could speak French. I've always hated Sundays.

THIRTEEN

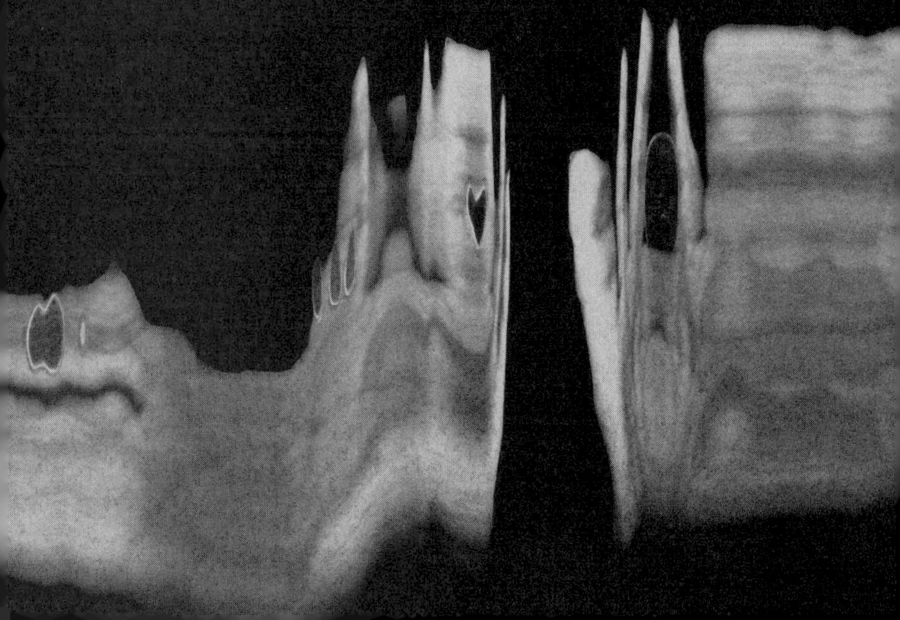

HOLLISTER WAS THE ONLY ONE I EVER TOLD. God knows why, because it wasn't a matter of selection, natural or otherwise. I mean it wasn't like I sat down and decided that this rich kid Hollister was the one to handle the stuff I was lugging around in an old valise held together by *plastique*.

I don't know. Maybe it was the beer or the weather patterns down in the Gulf. Maybe I just ran out of people to call when I didn't know where to go after the all-night theater. I forget how much we drank that day. Hollister had an ability to buy copious quantities of alcohol. His fake ID was excellent, his face mature; he carried himself well. He bought a cold case at the corner by the hot-dog stand, and we took it over to Wharton Manor.

Hollister wanted to investigate, to uncover something about my past. I didn't want to go, not really, but he asked so sweetly. I think the real thing was that I had something to put to rest in that old house. And maybe it was meant to be, because he actually found a crowbar over at the house, just lying around. How, I'll never know, when none of us could ever find a single tool of any use. I watched him tear off the boards that covered the kitchen door. It was late afternoon, plenty of light still.

We stepped inside and I inhaled the air like an asthmatic who suddenly finds oxygen. There was a terrible, sorry smell in the kitchen. I told Hollister I wasn't sure if I wanted to see the rest of the house. So we stayed there and drank for a long time without going into the other rooms. I watched the dust swirl round his head in the window light where my mother used to stand. There was a certain comfort in being around Hollister.

I leaned into one of the old counters, trying not to think about my mother, trying not to see her in the kitchen with us.

—I'm taking off for Europe after I graduate, he said.

—Why tell me about it, Hollister?

I mean there I was, an ex-patriot without so much as passage to the next port of call; why I'd want to hear about his parents sending him first-class to Europe, I couldn't fathom.

—You didn't think I'd leave you here? he laughed, sailing an empty beer can into the sink.

I pulled open a cabinet, just a nervous thing to do, and I was startled to find it full. Canned goods, sugar, a fresh sack of flour. More groceries than we ever had. My sister had told me, just a couple of weeks before this, that she'd had the place gutted.

—You're such a shit. I'm sure your folks would love that, I said.

I began a loud search for other dried goods, pots and pans, plates, silverware, paper towels. Not only weren't the drawers and shelves empty, there was a whole new supply of kitchen equipment. It was as if the physical body of the manor had seen the change of life coming and began to produce a sudden flurry of last-minute offspring. Deformed offspring crowding every vacant storage space.

—Who the fuck uses soufflé dishes? I said, holding two of them up for Hollister to consider.

—What makes you think I care what the old alkys think? he replied.

I threw open the door into the dining room. I wanted to get away from the discussion about Hollister's parents and their small-world concerns.

—Furniture! There's furniture! I shouted. A new table and a set of chairs to match, sideboards, hutches or whatever they're called, the kind of stuff my sister had in her apartment.

—Doesn't take much to please you, he said. He slipped in close to consider the dining room full of dining-room furniture.

—Jesus fucking Christ. Look at the living room. There's no way she sold the house this fast, I said. It had been less than a month since my mother had been taken to the hospice and I had gone to stay at Amanda's. I admit I didn't know a great deal about real estate at the time, but I thought it took longer than that just to get a house on the market.

There were two couches barely out of their packaging, armchairs, tables, lamps, books on shelves, a vase or two, the start of a collection—all to Amanda's style.

—But if she . . . sold it, why board it up? Hollister said. He stood behind me and slid his hands down my arms.

—A lot of the stuff in the kitchen is our old stuff, I said.

—Maybe she threw it in with the deal.

Hollister sank into the cushions of one of the couches and put his feet up on the coffee table.

There wasn't any way to take it all in. I was afraid to go upstairs. I knew no one was home, but I kept thinking I'd find another family there, another version of my family or just me, waiting in the dark of my mother's room.

I dropped into the couch next to Hollister. New-fabric fumes, stiff material. Hollister slipped his fingers into my blouse.

—A new couch deserves to be christened, he said.

But it was as if there was only air, not flesh, where he touched. I guess it really isn't fair to compare men—their flattering ways, their urgency, their anatomies. You do anyway. I began to make out with Hollister, but I was thinking about Nathaniel. Always thinking about Nathaniel no matter who I was with. That was the problem; I can see that now. They all fell short. They were too tangible, too physical. They sweated and carried viruses and stank of closed-off lives, mothers and fathers, institutions, all the things that molded them, that gave them form. But Nathaniel was more like the water main breaking under my house. He was pressure and force, my hands searching for a safe place to hold on, everything smashing up inside, the windows busting out, furniture dancing, the floor going weak and collapsing.

I stopped before things went too far.

—I have the clap, Hollister. I probably already gave it to you . . . before I knew. I'm sorry.

—I don't care. We can be treated at the same time, he said.

Maybe it was the mad air of the house that night or the way I almost blacked out doing it with him on the floor of the ballroom, or the sounds I imagined coming from the back of the house as if someone couldn't stop running water. But something changed.

When I came to, Hollister was talking to me. He looked like a man falling past an airplane window. I couldn't really hear him at first, but I saw his lips move in an animated way.

—Wait, I'll show you, I finally heard him say.

Hollister went off to another room, and for the first time I saw myself in one of the long ballroom mirrors in the half-light from the moon. I was a naked specter, dropped into the wrong time, the wrong century, the wrong family. A feral child, my hair frightened into a state, my body damp, hands curled in on themselves.

Maybe that was the only way I could move freely through the manor at that point, disconnected, turned half to animal. I climbed the wide sweep of stairs to the second floor. My room was the first on the left.

There was my old bed stripped the way a hospital bed is stripped when someone dies, two brand-new sets of sheets still in their packaging, placed with care on the mattress. My row of dressers stood at one end, but the drawers were empty, wiped clean. The closet held only hangers in that stark motel way that a closet can have. I was sick to think my history had been eliminated so thoroughly. All along I had assumed, at some point, when things calmed down between Amanda and me, she'd bring me back to the house and I'd get a chance to go through my possessions. I think I was even more amazed to see that the windows had been washed. I had never seen them washed before. And when I looked out at the garden, I discovered that at the corner of the property farthest from the house, a serious effort was underway to remove decades of weeds and bramble; the old fountain had been cleaned and drained. The window was halfway up. I could smell Amanda everywhere.

My mother's room was down the hall on the other side. At first I thought that all of her furniture had been replaced. Instead of her old double bed, a brand-new king-sized box spring and mattress, again with unopened packages of linen resting on top. New lamps, new easy chair. But there was her old dressing table, emptied, waiting for new bottles and brushes to touch down, to take over. In both of these rooms, the best pieces of furniture had been kept, the most endearing.

By the time I reached Amanda's room there wasn't any doubt left that she had begun the great effort to expand her territory. All of her old things were in place but newly arranged and dusted. And in the closet, dresses and jackets I knew she had worn just days before, back from the cleaners, hanging neatly.

I ran down the back stairs as if I was throwing myself to the bottom. I went through the pantry door and I slipped my hand into the crevice between the two cabinets. My body trembled the way my mother's did when she came out of surgery. I felt the keys.

I unlocked Mr. Graf's side of the house.

That's when I became conscious of Hollister. He had come up behind me and was watching as I threw the door open to the last of Mr. Graf's empty rooms—the one he used to inhabit.

—I was trying to find you everywhere, Hollister said.

—He's gone, I said, as if I still just couldn't believe it.

—Who's gone?

I let Hollister take my hand and he led me back to the other side of the house. We sat for a while on that couch in the living room again. I let him dress me and wash my face. He combed my hair and spoke to me in a quiet voice, and finally he took me away.

For Hollister, the manor was a dream arcade, everything his own reality could never be; maybe that's what attracted him to me, though it could have been the other way around.

We gathered our things and he did a half-ass job of boarding up the house again. Then we got in his car and drove for a long time. Hollister suggested we stop for a meal. He was big on meals. It occurred to me that he may someday turn his parents' alcoholism into a breathtaking ability to eat. But we all get fat with problems one way or another.

He picked a quiet coffee shop, the kind of place so nondescript you can't help but be put at ease. Hollister was being pretty nice about things, so I ate to keep him company.

—This is what I wanted to show you, he said, pulling something from his jacket. It was a passport. The name inside was Alice Hollister.

—She's just three years older than you, he said.

I guess we bore some vague resemblance.

—All you have to do is return to your natural color, cut your hair short, wear a pair of glasses.

And draw my lips together as if I'm frightened of something, I thought.

I thumbed through the passport. Pages covered with stamps. Hollister's sister was a traveler. I tried to hand it back to him but he pushed it across the table.

—It's a present, he said.

—You don't think she'll miss this? I said, trying to force it back his way against the pressure of his hand.

—She's taken a job working for a political campaign. She'll be sitting tight in the good old USA for at least a year; she won't even think about it. By the time they catch up with us, I'll have the whole thing straightened out.

—What whole thing straightened out? I said.

I could never comprehend Hollister's trust fund, any more than I could understand French politics, but it seems he had come into his own upon turning eighteen. "His own," it turned out, was the primary source of his family's own. He wouldn't have to fret over his passage or whether his mother understood him when she held up her bourbon and saw him waver through her ice cubes.

—Of course . . . if you should become the mother of the next heir . . . all would be forgiven, he said.

I think the thing I liked about Hollister was his rich fantasy life. I kissed him, like anything was possible. Then, over the quiet burn of coffee freshly made, I told him the entire story.

It's funny the way we remember. I go through a series of events, counting backward, watching a movie in reverse, but I've often resisted returning to the year of Mr. Graf.

I was looking out Amanda's bedroom window. I knew she had "Tribune" penciled in on the calendar on the refrigerator downstairs, her after-school job. She was a copygirl who liked to put in extra hours and go out with people from the paper—probably just the copyboys at first. Friday nights always ran long.

I'm sure my mother checked the same refrigerator calendar before making her plans. She must have figured I was in for the long wait for a rush-hour bus; I had the habit of staying at school late on Fridays to see if I could get my homework done in the library. I hated lugging all those hardbound books on the bus.

But it was the beginning of spring break and I came home early with little to do. I went into my sister's room and inhaled the satisfaction of knowing how much this would piss her off. I bothered her little tea set lined up on her window sill. It was the most incongruous thing about Amanda, the little-girl things. She was so busy creating an adult hysteria around herself then. Arranging for our boarder, seeing that Mother got better estimates for the house repairs, creating a budget that no one could really live with, reminding me of dental appointments, even nagging me to wash my hair.

I stood at her window with one of my mother's pilfered cigarettes in my fingers, lifted the miniature porcelain teapot lid and blew smoke inside. Polluting everything with my presence. I was watching for the smoke to waver out the tiny spout when I caught a glimpse of someone moving down in the garden. Amanda's favorite lavender teapot—supposedly a gift from our father one Christmas—fell to the floor and shattered.

I prayed it was Mr. Graf but it was only my mother. She was going up the back steps, dressed up in yet another new outfit. She wore new heels and I could only imagine enough perfume to exterminate the mosquito population spawning in our dead pond.

When she got right to the door, she disappeared from view under the eaves. I shut my eyes and heard the knock. The back door opened and closed. I kicked off my shoes and inched down the hall.

The key was in the usual place and I quickly slipped from our side of the house to the maids' quarters. There was Mr. Graf's room, the light pouring out from the crack under his door. The other rooms stiff with emptiness, the bathroom door ajar as always, the same single, limp towel draped over the rack, the tub clean and dry.

I just didn't give a shit anymore if I was caught. Mr. Graf could grab me with his bony fingers and tie me to a chair and hypnotize me into becoming a child slave, and I wouldn't care. I was already a slave to the moods and miserable offspring of moods of Wharton Manor.

I heard Mr. Graf and my mother talking low. Something dropped or was thrown to the floor. As I moved closer, I could smell the perfume left behind in the hall, and I had this thought. I'm not sure where it came from really, but I thought if everyone in the house was lying down for Mr. Graf, I might as well join them. I stretched out on the floor and put my head near the door. I breathed the dust and saw shadows—feet, and more things falling to the floor.

It sounded as if my mother and Mr. Graf were both a little short of breath, as if they were ascending into the family side of the house somehow. But, again, all I could see were the shadows slipping over the floor, almost stretching into the floor. Mr. Graf talked in a strange, rhythmical way, the way people do in iron lungs.

—You have to remain—independent. That's the thing—

you've never understood. But it's necessary now—more than ever. You have to be—unattached, unencumbered. Especially—where I'm concerned. If you worry about—trusting people—you'll never be free.

More things shifted and fell in the room.

—I can't bear—the loneliness, my mother said.

She was crying when she said this. She kept repeating her words as if he couldn't quite hear her.

—You keep buying—into the status quo—the group-think. I keep telling you—there's no—collective—unconscious—it's all conscious—as hell—one big—collective plot—to make everyone think—alike, Mr. Graf said.

He began to yell at her.

—Sell the damn house—put the girls—in boarding school—get a handle on this. You have to create—your own country—for Christ's sake. Your own rich—internal country—and never leave.

Then the sound I feared the most. I thought he was beating my mother. I was prepared to throw myself against the door, but Mr. Graf hadn't bothered to lock his private sanctuary. What I saw took place in slow motion.

Mr. Graf and my mother were both naked, their backs to me, my mother bent over. He was behind her, lecturing and banging that large body layered with years of submission. And I realized what a small man Mr. Graf was. She was pushed up against a massive stack of books, propped against one wall between a desk and dresser. Some of the books had broken free from the pile and hit the floor. That was the sound I'd heard.

They turned toward me at the same time. I grabbed Mr. Graf's arm and tried to pull him off her.

My mother began to say: God, God.

It was as if she was trying to summon a magical presence to help her through this betrayal. I saw his erect penis, the first I'd ever seen. It wagged about and diminished. Finally, I looked him full in the face and recognized my father.

I thought about running, but I waited for them to say something. I hadn't seen my father in years. The State had pronounced him dead. We lived in a ruin on the edge of the world because he was dead.

My mother pulled the top sheet off the bed and wrapped it around herself, hoping to retreat to her bedroom. But my father went over to the door and closed it firmly. He took his pants from a hook on the back and started to dress. My mother sat down on the bed and looked at the floor. My father put on a freshly ironed shirt as if he were dressing for the start of any day. He poured himself a cup of coffee from a pot on a hot plate.

—Coffee? he said to me.

I just stared at him. He returned the pot to the coils. He had aged considerably. I recognized one of his old chairs from his former study, still in good shape. He sat down, as if the session had just begun, as if my mother and I were both his patients once again.

—I thought you were dead, I said. I was standing against the wall, close to the door, as if I had been pushed there by an unrecognizable force.

But I think I always knew. I think I knew from the first day my sister mentioned our new tenant.

My mother was the only one who felt my anger. My father was unaffected, unaltered.

—You're prettier than I imagined, he said, looking into his cup as if there was a frivolous message floating there, something he thought I'd like to read with him.

—I'd say you're uglier, I said.

He smiled, as if to show me my sorry ways with a single glance. Then he shrugged.

—You should have let us . . . me know you were alive.

My father started to laugh. He laughed for quite a while. Then he looked at the shrouded figure of my mother, moaning on his bed. Her head was almost bound in the sheets it was lowered so deep into her chest.

—You thought I was dead. He smiled.

But it wasn't a question, it was a wondrous discovery on his part—to realize how much my mother and Amanda had managed to keep from me.

He went over to my mother, took one corner of the sheet and tried to pull it away from her. She fell over on her side into the mattress, securing the sheet with her weight.

I could see he hated wrestling with her. He turned to me.

—I asked her to explain, he said and returned to his chair.

Out of my father's bedding, my mother's smallest voice said: Amanda begged me not to tell.

My father shook his head at the pathetic nation of women he had raised. Then he said, more to himself than to anyone else: Amanda. Always in charge.

—So whose game is this? Amanda's or yours? I asked.

—You've left your mother out, he said.

My father looked toward the ceiling and stroked his mouth. I thought he was trying to come up with the best way to explain things, but all he was doing was trying to remember where he'd buried a certain envelope. He finally pulled it from the bottom drawer of the one dresser in the room, under shirts I knew my mother had pressed for him. He threw the envelope at the shape of my mother. Her body flinched.

I lifted the envelope off her and returned to my place by the door. Inside were newspaper articles written after my father's disappearance. The first few were fairly sensational items about a well-known psychologist's disappearance. A professional who left with a full calendar of appointments for the month to come. I had seen these before. Either my mother or Amanda had shown them to me.

I was about to hand the envelope back to him when I glanced at the next batch, written a few months later. It seemed, several women had pressed charges against my father, even though they knew he might never be found. Four women claimed he had seduced them while they were patients, causing irreparable damage. They were, they said, at their most vulnerable during that time, coping with personal crises for which they had turned to him for help and protection.

—It's true, isn't it? I said.

—You were an unhappy child. And you'll be an unhappy adult unless you learn to shift the focus of your concerns, he said.

My mother stood then and gathered the sheets about her. She went to her room with no one to hamper her way. I remained and watched my father get out a suitcase from under the small desk in the room. He began to pack his things. I guessed there was enough disturbance in the air at that point to send him on his way.

I had a million hates with no one to will them to. I looked at my father's uneager expression and realized there never had been any scientific experiments in his rooms, no apparatus. My father was just one of those cheap stage hypnotists making fools out of his audience. He had made us cluck like chickens, eat raw onions as if they were apples, cry every time we heard something funny, take off our shoes and try to give them to total strangers on the street.

I turned to leave.

—It wasn't so bad when it was just Mr. Graf over here, was it?

There was nothing I could say to that. If we're born as secrets partially told, my father was leaving again, without attempting to discover mine.

I'm certain my mother, Amanda, and I all believed my father guilty of the crimes with which he was charged. But I don't think Amanda felt she was doing anything wrong in sheltering him. For her, there would be something noble in forgiving such a wretch, honoring one of those egregious commandments despite everything. To that degree, she was probably more compassionate than any of us in the end. And perhaps she had been kind to hide the truth about our father from me for as long as she had, which might have given her a benign disposition if she'd started with a better personality from the first. But we always had to witness the worst of Amanda, to feel the full force of each blow.

Amanda had a sick stomach or something that day and came home early as well. When I left Mr. Graf's room, I saw her standing in the doorway, between the two parts of the house. She said nothing and stood aside to let me pass. Then she rushed down to his room.

Within minutes the fight began—maybe the worst one she and my mother ever had. Most of it has been wiped from my mind with a mercy cloth. I do remember Amanda screaming that Mom had blown everything. EVERY-THING! And for the first time I heard my mother raise her voice to equal measure.

—I've spent years ridding myself of that miserable creature. It's your goddamn fault I've become your father's hostage again! she screamed.

But there wasn't a word—not so much as the heat from a single one of their words—said to or about me that night. Only the fleeting vision of Amanda standing in my open bedroom door, backlit by the hall lamp.

She said: You owe me one very rare, very valuable lavender tea set.

I'm sure she just liked to say he gave it to her. I couldn't imagine him giving anyone a gift on Christmas, even if Amanda was his favorite. You see, he was the one who refused to celebrate holidays, making us all stand in his office to get a lecture on the promotion of holidays as advertising gimmicks. He railed against my mother for the simplest efforts at good cheer, the single strand of lights, the smallest wrapped present.

It was the power of that second leaving that forced everything else out of that year. Like the winter of a nuclear explosion—nothing else could carry much significance after that—it was just dead trees and sick animals and boarded up villages as far as I could see. Except for losing my virginity, I guess, which came right before or right after. I think it was right after, but it doesn't really matter.

He drove a bicycle-powered ice cream cart and had only six flavors. A hand-lettered sign with half the words misspelled. I remember teasing him about CHOCOLOTE. I don't think he spoke much English. We did it in Amanda's secret garden house, on the mildewed rug, mosquitoes attacking us. He was too old for me; I realized that right away. I never came out of the house after that when I heard the frail ice cream music looking for the kids in the neighborhood.

FOURTEEN

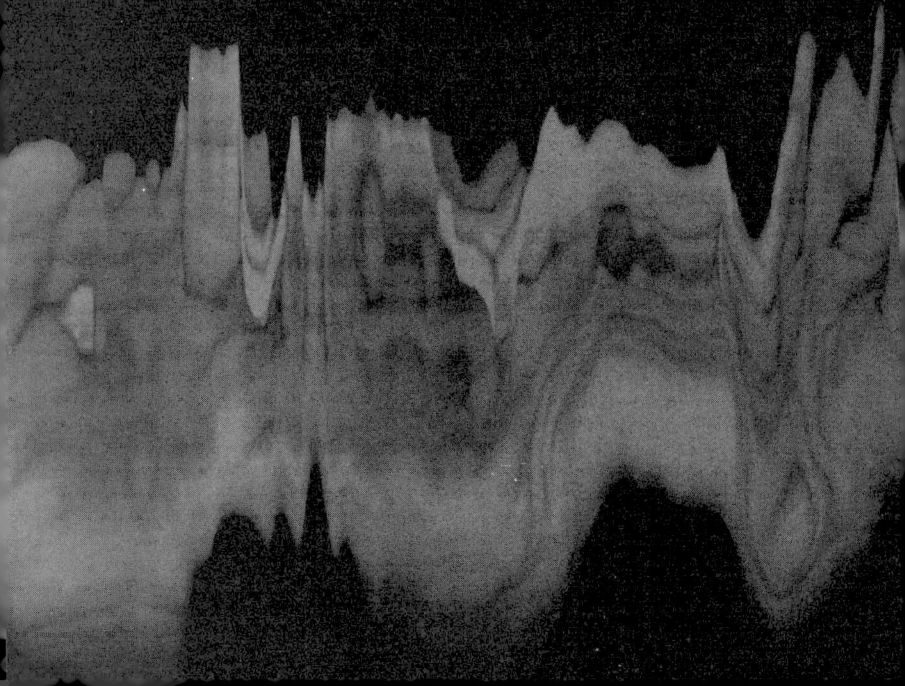

AFTER MY LONG CONFESSION, I MADE HOLLISTER DRIVE me out to the hospice again; he said he didn't mind. In fact, he said he wanted to. There I discovered that my mother's window screen had been driven into place with a lifetime supply of screws. It was secured beyond my prying fingers, my lack of tools. The feeling of stark daylight everywhere. I walked around to the entrance and went to the front desk. The pictures I'd cut from my mother's art books were in a tight, nervous roll. I drew them out of the backpack and flattened them against my stomach while I asked to see my mother.

She was, the two nurses told me, heavily sedated. I should let her rest as much as possible; limit my visit to fifteen minutes, no more. Reluctantly, they lent me a roll of masking tape but spent considerable time telling me where I shouldn't hang my pictures. One of them, the nurse in greatest authority, her glasses sitting upside down on her face, said: It's awfully nice of you to bring pictures. You know, *someone* stole the artwork from your mother's room the other night.

The young nurse looked embarrassed, apologetic.

But I let it pass; you can't hold onto everything.

My mother was asleep when I opened her door, or in such a lost drug place that she was in a false sleep, which worked almost as well. I didn't have the heart to try to pull her back to that room even when I had the pictures up—working over all the forbidden space with my masking tape.

You wonder where the dead go, and you wonder where the living go when they're looking for them. Because that's where my mother was, off somewhere looking for the dead. When I think back, I like to imagine that she opened her eyes after I left that day and traveled for a time inside a favorite painting again.

I can't help wondering about her own paintings, because I do have a loose memory or two of a time when I was very small and I thought she painted. So much energy around my father's dead and costly books, but no one ever tried to imagine where my mother's work was buried.

There's a face . . . I still think I can see it on her easel. But maybe I never saw it; maybe it was just something formed of her stories. Anyway, there's a face. Like my mother but made of vibrant, slender lines. A light coming in from a window, spotting the floor where she works, a mirror on the far wall. I don't even remember the room, just the floor and the mirror and the face on the easel, for some reason more visible than my mother's face just now.

Then my father in front of her painting, blowing pipe smoke, making lye-and-acid remarks about the futility of art or her efforts. Maybe something about never achieving anything in the ivory-tower art market. He might have said she would always be a failure or her art would always be a failure or all art was by its nature a failure. Which takes me back to his game, his God-almighty game. Wondering what it was that we were all supposed to win. Certain that none of us ever had. Not even Amanda, his masterwork.

The nurses stopped back three times to coax me to leave. The last time it was the younger nurse, and she slowly took my arm. When I wept into my mother's face, I was relieved to find it still warm, almost hot.

As I lifted my head, I saw the nurse give an uncertain, sorry look at the reproductions on the wall. She said something uncomfortable about the head nurse and her stickler rules. It was her way of saying that art vanishes quickly in the world of the dying. And I said: They'll give her more comfort than anyone could.

But you can't argue with such efficiency.

A few hours later I called back; I had to talk with my mother. I felt so stupid to be right there without trying to wake her. There were too many things to sort out. I felt desperate, really. Crazy to be forgiven, insane to forgive. I explained this at length, as if the nurse on duty—someone different this time—needed to hear it, and I wouldn't let her interrupt even though she tried. But then, of course, I knew. I think most of us know about that kind of thing.

Because when she finally did get me to slow down, she said that my mother had died shortly after I left.

Some emotions are stronger than curiosity. You wonder about your mother's face, thinking you might have changed that expression of hers somehow. Even if you never could when she was alive. But you can't bring yourself to open the casket to find out. And now you watch as her casket is lowered with a loud winch into the earth. It's a kind of agreement to let her expression haunt you the rest of your life because you couldn't bring yourself to look.

But I never went to the funeral. Amanda took care of everything.

I spent the days that followed in a lost city. There's no memory game, no trick of the imagination I can conjure to retrieve those days, but then I wouldn't want to. I know I was with Hollister, but I couldn't say if we stayed with a friend of his or snuck into his parents' apartment or rented a hotel room downtown. That's how bad it was. I'm sure there were drugs. There were always drugs with Hollister, but I don't remember taking any. And maybe he saw me falling through every floor I tried to walk across, past every bed he tried to wrap me in. Or maybe I was watching him. He told me later that we did have a hotel suite for a while and that we both went to a clinic one afternoon and bravely took our penicillin. He also said I freaked out every time he ran the water in the bathroom, even to wash his hands.

I don't know why we get so loaded down with the wrong stuff, the least meaningful things. There I was, just emerging from Mom's death, handling the sentence about being an orphan in my head, wondering if I could face going back to Amanda's apartment to get my things, trying to figure how I was going to convince Nathaniel about the rightness of moving in with him, when I had to start thinking about the clap.

Even though I'd only been a minor player in a small and ignoble chain of events, like the fool who turns on a light switch and triggers the bad wiring throughout an entire three-story walk-up, I realized that any city can go up in flames a second time, despite my theories of a watery apocalypse.

Hollister and I were in a coffee shop when it hit me. We were sitting in a window booth, and he was kissing my fingers. He was ready to spend some time at home and was trying to figure out what to do with me until his graduation in another month and the trip he was planning for us. Hollister liked to sort things out. His newly acquired inheritance and authority glowed from his skin. I think any other woman would have been captivated; maybe I was a little.

I went back through the days, months really, trying to restore events, names, faces . . . strangers. I came up with some excuse to be off by myself for a while.

Hollister clung to me a long time. He wrapped me in his jacket outside the coffee shop and talked a soft babble about Paris. I know he was relieved to have a break. He gave me too much pocket money and said he'd come after me if I didn't call that night.

I did what I could to repair things. I made a bunch of calls. Maybe it was another form of intimacy. And maybe, in a way, it was better than the sex itself. I was amazed at how many of them I could find and how nice they were about it—well, most of them anyway.

The last time I saw Nathaniel he opened the door to his apartment, still in his pajamas, dried blood caked on his lip and chin, his T-shirt. In every way the disheveled man, in need of hot water, a change of clothes, food, coffee. He stank of old booze and new booze and bad events.

He didn't invite me in; he didn't see me out. He could hardly walk across the room.

I went into the kitchen to see if I could find some coffee. When I asked if he had any coffee filters or paper towels to use for filters, it was as if he finally realized I was in the apartment with him.

—Why don't you take a shower and I'll run and get you some breakfast down the street? I said.

—Ah, it's the little sister. The little sister of mercy, he said.

I went into his bathroom and started the shower. Then I came back to where he was slumped into a chair, clutching a nearly empty vodka bottle. I pulled on his arm to get him to follow me into the bathroom. The bottle slipped and drained out into the rug before he could catch it.

—Alright . . . you take a shower. I mean, I'll take a shower and you go hop like a little bunny and go get old Nathaniel another bottle of vodka, he said.

—Alright, I said. When I left, I realized the water would run the whole time I was gone and he'd still be there, on the toilet or down in the carpet, licking the fibers, sucking up the last of the vodka.

It took three stores until I could find someone willing to sell to me. When I got back, he was passed out on his bed. I turned off the shower. For a while I curled up next to him and fell asleep.

When I woke up, I tried to arouse him but it didn't work. I waited until he came to. It was pretty late by then. He didn't want my stinking offer to run down the block and get him coffee and breakfast. He didn't want me running the stinking shower again, or touching his stinking shoulders or head to ease the stinking pain.

—I'll come back later. We can talk then, I said, grabbing my purse and heading toward the door.

—Fucking talk. Your sister's done enough of that to last a lifetime.

I turned to look at my lover, diminished in his sour pajamas, his head massive, maybe from holding it roughly in his hands like the unwanted object it was. Most of the blood was gone from his face now, wiped into his skin.

—Amanda knows about us? I said.

—Shit, what kind of bastard do you . . . ? Don't answer that, he laughed in a useless way.

I thought that would be the end of it, but he said: I don't think she'd appreciate that little jewel just now.

—So . . . what about you and me? I said.

—Jesus Christ, I'm dying here. You and me what?

—Nothing, I said.

—Look, I'm sorry about your mother.

—Everything will change now, I said.

Although I didn't say it, I meant something about the way my mother had been so trapped. Body-and-soul trapped. And now Amanda had become trapped as well.

—You better run along, Molly.

—We've had our little game then? I whispered, everything caught in my throat—that emotion greater than curiosity.

—What? he said.

—You have the clap. You better tell Amanda, I said and shut the door behind me.

Terrible loves never leave you; I had to live with that. It was one of those things my mother taught me.

There was a day, somewhere between Mr. Graf's departure from Wharton Manor and the diagnosis of my mother's cancer when she and I went to the Art Institute. Amanda had gone off to college by then. My mother and I hardly knew how to find each other in such a big house after that.

But there was an afternoon when I heard Mom call in sick at her job and sneak out the front door. I caught up with her at the bus stop.

Though she was hardly pleased about it, she let me come along. My mother knew I could store up questions, though I'd probably never ask most of them, the way my father only unwrapped a fraction of the books he purchased. She feared the one question leading to the worst kind of knowledge.

We took the bus downtown and she looked out the window and I looked at her. It was another one of those springs made for tearing me apart. I slept with most of the boys in the neighborhood that season but never wanted to see them again after we did it. A couple of them got into fights, I heard.

Mom wanted to see the big Chagall windows that day, more than anything. I mean they are amazing, but it's like anything after a while, you have to get up and move into the next room. That day she wouldn't budge from the bench in front of those windows. She was caught in the blue light, paralyzed. I kept thinking, if she could open one of those windows, she'd leap from it, right then and there, and be rid of us all.

—Mom, I said.

—Shhh, she said.

—Mom, I have to ask you something.

—Don't spoil it, Moll.

—Were you glad when you found out who Mr. Graf was? I said.

At first I didn't think she was going to answer but she said: Your father is a remarkable man. Most men aren't, Molly.

Despite everything, she was still under his influence. She wouldn't say another word, though I tried to get her to for a long time. I pulled at her sleeve until I heard the threads strain. I called him every name in a low whisper. I threatened to run away. But she chose to ignore me. Instead, she ascended into the Chagall windows with the other figures, seeing herself, perhaps, as a bride floating with a light bouquet in her hands.

Hollister found an apartment for me. He made all the arrangements; I didn't follow most of it. The building was modern, on the Drive, toward downtown. I never thought I'd get used to it, but after a while I didn't mind having a doorman and a delivery entrance in my life.

It was supposed to be this great secret. But Hollister told Sharon; he knew she'd find out one way or another. Maybe it was that newfound charm of his, but she didn't tell anyone and somehow we got away with it.

Hollister was over most evenings, going back to his parents' place at night. Sometimes Sharon brought over one of her men. They'd spend an afternoon or a few nights in the spare bedroom together. I didn't mind.

All we really had to do was keep the noise down so the neighbors wouldn't ask after the aunt who was supposed to be the owner of the apartment—my new guardian.

Hollister had this thing about both of us graduating. He was very conscientious when he wasn't stoned out of his mind. He hired a tutor so I could get extra credits. He graduated in June and I actually finished up a couple of months later, after the summer session. My grades were trash, but then no one really expected any different, after my losing Mom.

One day, after I was settled in at the new apartment, I finally went over to get my things at Amanda's. It was on a Saturday. I didn't ask, but Nathaniel wasn't around. She appeared to be half moved out. All the shades were drawn, the curtains pulled in about themselves. We sat in her living room in a spare corner, her dark glasses in place.

She wore a black dress. It was easy to see, even with the glasses, that one of her eyes had been blackened. Nathaniel's work, no doubt.

—How appropriate, I said.

—What? she asked, as if I'd just pulled her back from a closet where she was crouched behind long coats. She took another strong belt of her drink and waited.

—That you're wearing black. It's quite becoming. You must have had to do a lot of shopping for the occasion, I said.

—I told myself we wouldn't do this today, Molly. I know we both have to calm down and figure out how we're going to deal with things from now on, she said, trying to keep her voice as even and steady as the booze in her glass.

She got up to cross the room to the latest cabinet where she was trying to hide the alcohol. I could smell Nathaniel all over her. Her nylons swished for him. Her heels dug into the carpet thinking about him. Her lips barely moved like she was talking more to him than me.

I still thought she'd tire of him after the worst of the guilt had a chance to wear off. I gave her the same fake smile she gave me. She sat down again.

—Help yourself if you want a Coke or something.

I didn't say anything. I was just there to make her nervous.

—I wish I'd had some way of getting in touch with you. I had to go ahead and make arrangements. I had her cremated. I think that's what she would have wanted. I appreciated that you called Edith. At least I didn't have to report you as a missing person.

I heard what she said. She called mother "her." Even when Mom was nothing but ash, she was still a distant pronoun.

I let it pass.

—Look, Molly, I should go over the plans with you.

—I'm not sure Mom wanted a memorial service . . . but she did pay for a burial plot. She told me about that. Can you come up with a plan to turn her back to a whole body again? You're such a wizard with the material world, I said.

Another glass was drained. She started in on vodka. Cold vodka that she got out of the refrigerator.

Then she leveled it on me: Molly, there's so much you don't know. I don't think you had any idea how bad her finances were. I tried. . . .

A lone tear ventured from her dark glasses.

—I had to stop paying for the cemetery plot when I was

in high school, Molly. And then, when all of this happened, I kept thinking about the dream I had. Remember? About us burying her under the ballroom floor? So I thought . . . if we had an urn of ashes . . . well . . . we'd be able to do just that. She always did love the ballroom; I think that's why she bought the house.

—And she'd be dancing on top of it right now if you hadn't rented out the rooms to Mr. Graf.

I never called him "father" after what happened. He was always Mr. Graf to me.

—Jesus, Molly, she said.

There were times when I'd just graze her with that unfathomable history of ours—and times when I'd come right out and ask why she kept Mr. Graf to herself that way. But Amanda would give me this look, like I was the worst kind of carnivore—not just willing, but eager to feed on her own. And that's as far as we'd ever get.

—He's the reason she got cancer, I said.

—No, he's the reason there was money for me to go to school—for you to go to college if you don't blow it.

—Well, I wouldn't want to blow it. Not if there's money at stake. You can bury my mother anywhere you please, I said, getting up to pack my things.

—We have to talk about the rest, Molly. We have to talk about Nathaniel.

I sat down again. I was ready now.

I went over and filled a glass with ice from the bucket and poured myself a drink, though I really couldn't stomach it. I let it sit and perspire into one of my sister's favorite tables, ignoring the coaster.

She told me they were getting married as soon as possible, and I didn't flinch. They had talked about where they wanted to live. She said they'd never get any money for the old house just then, so it made sense to move back in and remodel. It was even possible, with Nathaniel's influence in the building industry, that they could shake a few things up by way of urban renewal, turn a profit eventually.

I didn't tell her that I had been to Wharton Manor, that I had seen her plans made manifest.

—What a little triumph, I grinned.

—We'll buy out your half of the house, Molly.

Even under the sunglasses, I could see how much my sister's face began to relax and she loosened her grip on her glass when she set it down on the table.

—I hope you'll spend it on college abroad, she said.

I was about to tell her about Nathaniel, about my plans with Hollister, when she added: Then maybe you won't mind so much . . . about Father.

—About Mr. Graf, I said.

I actually thought she was about to beg my forgiveness for Mr. Graf—something she had never done. But I didn't realize how intently she was looking to the future, sorting out her new plans, her vivid life.

—He got in touch with me recently, she said.

I just didn't get it at first.

—Has he ever been out of touch with you? Even when he was dead he kept in touch with you, I said.

She looked away and said: I'm not going into it right now. But Nathaniel and I agree the best thing is to let him stay at the house for a while with us. It's funny . . . but he wants the maids' rooms again. You'd think. . . . Maybe some people never change.

My sister hated it when I laughed at her. And this time, I just let loose. I rolled with laughter. Screamed. Howled. He hadn't left after all. Not for any real length of time, not out of her psyche.

I laughed so hard I forgot about packing my clothes, the old family photographs, the few possessions. I left and let the door shut by itself.

I could hear her shouting after me, all the way down the stairs, out the two front doors, into the street, and out of her country.

FIFTEEN

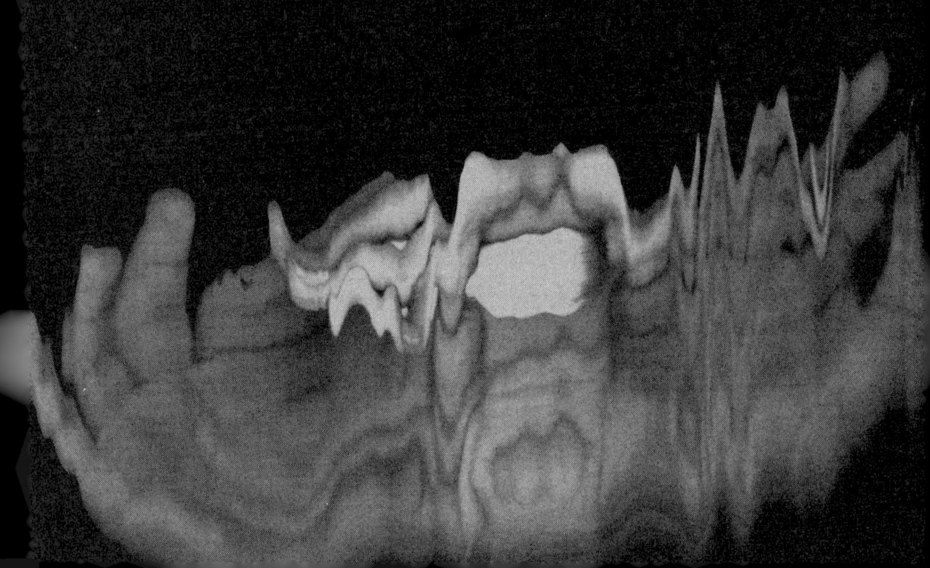

WE HAD BEEN IN PARIS FOR NEARLY A YEAR WHEN Sharon came over for a few weeks. She stopped in to see me one day when Hollister was out. She looked thinner than I remembered and smoked twice as much.

—My doctor's giving me this incredible combination of diet pills, Sharon said. She glanced at her legs while she thumbed through the French *Vogue* on our coffee table.

—The ones that give you a heart attack?

—Wouldn't it be a great way to go? As soon as the baby comes I'll send a bottle over and you can try them, she said.

Sharon never did understand her own sense of humor. She stretched and walked over to the small balcony overlooking the city. Hollister had managed to find us a place with a perilous view—a million rooftops, serene gardens. I don't think Sharon noticed—she was raised on perilous views. She leaned into the doorjamb as if she was working her body for an invisible camera. She didn't have any real plans yet. Paris was just filling time for a while.

—Open the package, Molly, Sharon said.

While she waited, her body swayed toward the late afternoon, flirting with the skyline. It was something from Sharon's parents. I got the ribbon off, lifted one corner of the box and peeked inside. More pink stuff. I threw it onto the ever-growing pile of baby items that arrived daily from Hollister's family friends with names meant to impress, but at least amused me. Tiny bathrobes with matching, hand-stitched towels, the world's most expensive rubber ducks. Each darling little thing made me feel like a woman choking on bonbons, smothering under soft blankets, dying at the hands of teddy bears, giraffes, and elephants.

We both watched in silence as it hit the pile and the miniature outfit slid out of the box to the floor. Sharon returned to the couch across from me and lit a skinny black cigar with pink edging.

—You shouldn't wait too long to get married, Molly.

I rang for the maid so she could top off our coffees and straighten the gifts again, which she spent far too much of her time doing.

Sharon reached for the sugar on the silver tray.

—You'll never be completely at home in Hollister's

set—it's just the way it is—but there's a certain tolerance people have. . . . Unless, of course, you're talking bastard children; we just give up at that point.

—Croissant? I asked.

When Sharon couldn't get anywhere with me, she told me about a baby born with a harelip who could predict the weather and the stock market. And babies born with their spines sticking out of their backs like tails. And babies . . . well, I stopped listening about babies after a while.

She finished with: I insist on being a godmother, you know. A frightening prospect for both of us. She kissed me on both cheeks and left me swimming in layers of buttery pastry. I think we parted on friendly terms.

Paris isn't bad; better than I expected. Hollister's happy here. He hopes I'll fall completely in love with the city, that we'll be here forever.

For a while we did nothing but wander through museums, but I don't seem to have the energy for it now. So mostly we take taxis and eat tons of little meals. We go out with friends; he seems to be thick in expats. And we meet lots of Parisians who hate the fact that my command of their language is atrocious and that I don't seem to gravitate toward improvement.

Everything got straightened out about the passports and visas and stuff; I never asked Hollister how he pulled it off. They are, it seems, a more influential family than I understood them to be. I know his mother was upset until she got the news that I was going to have her grandchild.

Now they're talking about coming over for a visit soon. I've threatened to take off if they do. But I might quiet down.

I didn't plan to get pregnant. I was worse than distracted. By the time I realized I was, well, it gets to be a pretty serious operation this far into it. I have this paralyzing fear of foreign doctors and their medical facilities. I won't even get my teeth cleaned over here, which makes Hollister crazy. It took forever to convince me I should see a French gynecologist for regular checkups. (Big knuckles, all of them.)

The baby is his. I've been weary of men in general for some time; their strange meeting places, their unrelenting desires, their foul habits. Though there is something about the idea of doing it with a guy when you can't understand him, can't even translate. The trouble is, so many of them, so very many of them, are unremarkable.

Hollister keeps saying we should get married. I guess he worries about the heir thing. But I'm not sure.

I did get a brief letter from Amanda. She wrote about the manor mostly, the fine points of remodeling. She hardly mentioned Nathaniel, nothing about Mr. Graf. It seemed like a waste of time answering her. I mean, what do you say? "Glad to hear it's going so well"? I did call Edith before I left town. I told her to tell Amanda that she could take my half of Wharton Manor and put it in a bank account under my name and send me the bankbook. Most of the time, I try not to think about her, and if Hollister ever brings her up, I make an effort to refer to her in the past tense.

But a couple of nights ago Hollister came in around

three A.M., a little wasted, much too cheery, and we ended up talking for a while. I had encouraged him to go out; I needed time to myself, to formulate the plan I'm working on. He found me lying on the bed without any covers, my eyes open, one dim light fading in the corner of the room.

—Waiting up for me? Or just waiting for more baby things to arrive? he said.

He was filled with one of his maddening urges to get close to me. I could feel it in his hands as he dropped onto the bed and rubbed my back.

—How was it out there tonight? I said.

Hollister named a café, people I didn't know.

—Did you spend the night telling your new lover about your weird pregnant girlfriend? The one who resides in your dark Paris apartment? I said.

—I know you can't stand to hear me say it, but I don't even think about other women.

I guess no one ever told Hollister there's no better way to lose someone. I rolled over so he'd stop gripping my nightgown and thought about ringing for something to eat, but I couldn't decide what I wanted; I was getting tired of confections. After a while we turned on the television and got the maid up. She made us a variety of breakfast foods, all presented tastefully on little plates.

Hollister and I curled into bed after she straightened all of the covers and sheets again. She changes them once a day so they are always inviting, kind to the skin.

Maybe I'll stay with Hollister, for a while anyway. I'd prefer that he wouldn't get so captivated with things, but I guess I can put up with that. And though it's amusing about never fitting, never quite belonging in the stunning set—as Sharon so kindly pointed out—that wouldn't keep me from sticking. When I leave, it will be about something urgent that has nothing to do with Hollister.

I looked at the poor man twisting his fingers into the sheets, his anxious looks at my belly, and kissed him on the cheek. Without really meaning to, I began to tell him about my last meeting with Amanda. I even told him that I almost cracked up over Nathaniel. But I was sorry as soon as the words were out of my mouth; there wasn't any reason to hurt him that way.

I got out of bed. Hollister followed. He grabbed my arm and held on with some force.

—You didn't tell your sister about having an affair with her boyfriend? he said.

He let my arm go, probably worried about cutting off the baby's circulation. But I was surprised to see this pleased expression come over him. Then he hugged me around the thick middle and said: You're too wonderful.

If it was a joke I didn't get it and told him so.

—That was probably the only moral thing you've ever done in your entire life, Molly, he laughed.

I've actually thought about that for a long time now, why I didn't tell Amanda, and I'm not so sure Hollister's right.

—Maybe it was just a sense of . . . knowing, I said.

—Knowing what?

—That life was prepared to take care of its own for a change. I mean I was sitting with my sister, watching the booze take over, watching the spiders crawl up her windows and look for a crack to slide through, and I had this clear vision of her future.

Hollister lit a cigarette and sat down at my dressing table to listen.

—You see, she'll have this big old house full of mother-guilt to live in. The plumbing and wiring and sewage systems will break down constantly. And one day things will just go.

—Go? he said, pulling a sliver of tobacco from his tongue.

—By fire or water or insects; it really won't matter. What will matter is that on the day it happens she'll call out to her father for help. After all those years of caretaking and hiding him, she'll be devastated when he reaches for his suitcase and walks out the back door, leaving his impenetrable library behind. And, in desperation, she'll call out to Nathaniel.

What I didn't tell Hollister was that Nathaniel will be in a stupor on the living-room couch, dreaming of the woman who made his heart leap from balconies and fast-moving taxicabs.

—When he hears her frantic voice, he'll pull himself together just enough to wander out the front door, wondering why he ever thought their marriage would work.

I can see the house collapsing. It will start with the kitchen and move up the back stairs when it goes.

—Amanda will get a phone call from her boss, who'll say the media attention surrounding her and her father has made it too difficult to keep her on at the magazine. She'll put the phone down, and that's when she'll think about me in Paris with you and the child she wanted, the endless rooftops. . . .

—But you still could have told her as a parting shot. Or sent her a telegram; we've been here for months. That's what I'm saying. In the end, you were generous with Amanda.

I didn't know what to say.

Besides, I have other things to think about just now. I actually told Hollister some of it that night. I took a handbill from the bedside table to show him, an advertisement someone left at a small restaurant where I dined one day.

Dr. P. T. Givens—it proclaimed—was the world's foremost authority on hypnotism. His list of credits so long it barely fit on the goldenrod paper. His face smooth and pleasing. The kind of person you felt you knew instinctively.

—He holds full professorships at Harvard and Tulane? Hollister scoffed.

—Dr. Givens is seeking a select group to train in his technique, I said, looking past the television, out toward the morning sky.

—A select group of suckers, Hollister chuckled lightly.

Pregnancy is nothing if not dramatic. When he saw my face, he quickly changed.

—My entire future hinges on taking this course, Hollister.

I began to weep.

—Honest to God, anything you want, he said. Anything.

I guess I didn't tell Hollister why my future would be in peril without Dr. Givens, because it isn't about me. The plain truth of it is, once I become proficient, I'll be able to start from the first. Not to work on my daughter's memory. Memory is such a hideous thing. And not to convince her, even in the subtlest way, of something foolish or overpublicized, like happiness or generosity. But you can hypnotize someone into believing that her life is her own. That's all I want for her; that she will grow up with the conviction that life is hers.

There was little point, that morning, in telling Hollister I'd already spoken with Dr. Givens over the phone and made arrangements to start. Though the course of study will be held in Paris, he said it doesn't matter that I don't speak French; it turns out he instructs primarily in English and, in case I had any friends who speak mostly French, he works very closely with a full-time translator.

Dr. Givens expressed, in an almost tender way, that after I complete my studies and sit for the exam, I'll be able to get a license. I'll have my own clients and my own income, and a handsome one at that, he said.

Before I got off the phone, I asked him if I'd be able to practice in any country, since I really wasn't sure where my daughter and I would be. Dr. Givens laughed encouragingly. He said he understood the expatriate life all too well. There was absolutely nothing for me to worry about, he assured me. Nothing in the least.